I0596903

Sullivan House

Sullivan House

A. M. CRANE

SULLIVAN HOUSE
by A. M. Crane

Copyright ©2017 by A. M. Crane All rights reserved. This book or part thereof may not be reproduced in any form by any means, electronic or mechanical, including photocopy, recording, or otherwise, or by any information storage and retrieval system, except as may be expressly permitted in writing from the publisher as provided by the United States of America copyright law. Requests for permission should be addressed to Doce Blant Publishing, Attn: Rights and Permissions Dept., 32565-B Golden Lantern St. #323, Dana Point, CA 92629

Published by Doce Blant Publishing, Dana Point, CA 92629

www.doceblant.com

Cover art by Fiona Jayde Media
Interior Design by The Deliberate Page
Edited by K. H. Koehler

Hardbound ISBN-13: 978-0-9994937-7-9
Paperback ISBN-13: 978-0-9994937-8-6
Digital ISBN-13: 978-0-9994937-9-3

Printed in the United States of America
Library of Congress Control Number: 2017956672

The Sullivan House is a work of fiction. Names, characters, places and events are the product of the author's imagination and/or are used fictitiously. Any resemblance to actual persons, living or dead, including events and locations, is entirely by coincidence.

Special thanks to Mark Angeloni.

For my sister, Shari.

I will not look on you with pity; I will not spare you.
I will surely repay you for your conduct and for the
detestable practices among you. Then you will know
that I am the LORD.

(Ezekiel 7:4)

PROLOGUE

Near the place that would become Savannah, Georgia – 1693

BLOOD DRIPPED DOWN THE LENGTH of his thread-bare tunic. His trembling hand reached for his left cheek, and there he felt the skin warm and sticky. Something razor-sharp had caught him there, grazing the skin just above his jowls. He'd turned his head to catch sight of the predator but found nothing, only the ravages of the creature that had sliced his skin. As if to reassure himself, the thought crossed his mind: *It probably saved your life, Eli. You turned your head in the nick of time and saved your throat.* He found no comfort in this.

A branch cracked. He turned his head and saw the tree with limbs the size of Roman colonnades. Wood splinters displaced the dirt at his feet. He picked up his pace and ran faster than was normally possible, given the ill-fitting sandals tied about his bloodied feet. Only once did he trip over the cassock that dragged about his ankles. It had torn long ago to leave his legs bare and vulnerable.

The priest ducked as he fled beneath a low-lying limb and dropped the hood to unveil his face. Autumn was nearly past, and the leaves that were still turning color would meet a bitter end. Thankfully, most had fallen to the ground. Beyond the tree line, a dense mist crept slowly with tendrils that reached with claw-like fingers over the ground.

"*Quaero qui cecidisti.*"

The voice was not human, a whispered call from an ethereal host. It hissed, and the monk's spine felt the chill.

"*Eli.*"

Something wanted him. *It knows my name! It seeks me out.* There was no way to soften his footsteps over the crispness of dried dead leaves, so he did not try. Instead, he ran. To one side, a cyclone of debris and underbrush rose as something passed by faster than the eye could track. Eli quickly scanned the brush for any signs of the predator but found nothing as the gust settled and fell silent. The mist followed, and another slice of his forearm sent fire up to his chest. He quickly glanced at the damage, afraid of what he might find, and saw dirt and bits of bramble stuck to his flesh. He brushed it off and silently cursed the dense forest.

"Oh, my Father, please…" Eli cried out with fists clasped in prayer. Blood drizzled between his knuckles, and the mist hissed at it. He set off again, this time in the opposite direction. The mist followed. He dared not look behind as he ran, certain that the predator clung to his heels. It lived in the mist—a vapor that breathed, lived, and hunted him.

"Holy Mother…"

He dodged a low-lying branch but caught his foot in the dense vines that snaked from tree to tree. Some seemed to move in serpentine slithers only when his eyes were focused elsewhere—a subtle shift seen only with a peripheral glance. Eli scrambled to his knees, and his lips began to move rapidly.

"Oh, God in Heaven, if nothing else, let me survive, and I'll be thy eternal servant, sacrificing all I have—my very soul, if need be."

Eli lifted his head and opened his eyes, hopeful that some deity had received his prayer. Ahead, the flicker of light played against the thicket. Somewhere, there was life in this place, where he had only seen Death's gaping jaws waiting to be fed.

You must have faith, Eli, he thought, berating himself in silence. Indeed, wasn't it his job as a priest to oversee the rites of those just fallen—to pray over the dead? There were no dead here, not yet anyway. Even still, his heart told him otherwise. As if to sanction his thoughts, the mist crawled forward, and a ghostly voice laughed hideously within it.

You have become prey.

He stood upright and began to run again. If he could make the clearing, he might be safe. At least he could scream for help, and perhaps that alone would save him. *If someone hears me, they'll come. Surely, they'll come save me.* He longed for a new surge of hope, but his gut recoiled.

He blinked and once more bargained with God to spare his life, promising anything—everything—in exchange, and vowed to keep his eyes focused on the flickering light as a witness of his faith. Its glow danced, shadowed by something that crossed between him and the torches. It passed, and whispered laughter, high and melodic, echoed from the trees. The predator toyed with him.

He turned off the path and darted off to his left, hoping to avoid whatever owned the shadow that lay between him and the light. *Fool! Foolish man, you are!* He cursed himself again in gasped words. His breath heaved against his ribs and came out in grunts. There was no possible way to stay silent now, no way to hide. He simply had to outrun it—this thing that pursued him. He turned his head and searched the trees for the light but could see nothing—except the pulsing vapor.

At that moment, a fiery barb knifed its way into his neck. White-hot flame seared his veins and instantly paralyzed his body. He wanted to cry out in agony, but instead, gurgled blood. He opened his eyes and saw only vapor and shadows. *I will indeed die.* The thought suddenly gave strength to his weakened limbs and propelled him to his feet. He scrambled for the clearing.

"I believe in the Holy Spirit…" The monk's voice gurgled in his throat. "…the holy Catholic Church, the communion of saints…"

Suddenly, the canopy opened, and a brilliant full moon showered silver light across an open field. Ahead, a single flame flickered through glass.

"Oh, thank you, Father…"

Eli stumbled forward—his feet unable to feel the grass beneath him. Heaving his broken body through the mead, his vision was suddenly clouded by looming obscurities that towered overhead and eclipsed the moonlight. Tall iron gates to either side pierced the night sky with spikes that crowned the top of each spear. Within individual barbed iron clusters, a pillar of stone had been erected and capped with a single creature carved out of onyx. Blank eyes stared over a gaping mouth that dripped with fangs waiting to pierce its next victim. A single tail encircled the capstone in giant ropes. The entire monument, a wolfish beast that grasped hold of the pillar with four bared claws for feet, seemed to move.

Gargoyles, he supposed, then corrected his thoughts. *No, not gargoyles. There is no water. Those are grotesques, meant to be the watch-keepers, protectors.* Eli glanced at the grotesques carved for protection and sensed there would be none.

As he crawled past the gates, he saw the grounds were withered with abandoned shrubbery that had once belonged to a Lord or Lady's garden. Blank eyes watched him and stone creaked as the onyx heads turned to watch Eli enter. Overlooking the curvature of what once was a great porte-cochere, murky walls rose in peaks and turrets spotted with the same stone grotesques. Thirteen junctions became their perch, and as they watched Eli, their inky eyes glistened.

Overhead, yawning holes for windows, filled with opaque glass, seemed to gape at the helpless monk. These were the only windows to face the front of the estate. A few empty spaces twisted to face the embankments of the expansive grounds.

"A house," Eli whispered in thanks. "Perhaps those with faith dwell there."

A single candle flickered in a lone window on the first floor—the light Eli had seen from the forest. Its glint lured him the way a moth flies to a flame.

He moved toward it.

A set of steps rose to the grand entryway. Behind an oddly burnished veranda, there were two vast, ornately carved, mahogany doors on bronze hinges.

Behind, on the grounds, the vapor curled around a pair of sentry gates and began to crawl toward him. Eli clamored up the stairs and, gasping for breath, rolled onto the entry deck. To one side, the candle flickered as, suddenly, the mist called out once more.

"Eli."

He rolled back to his hands and knees and mouthed supplication. Pain racked his body and opened his senses. Abruptly, Eli stopped, panting. His eyes fixed on something ahead.

"Sweet Lord, help me!"

One of the entry doors stood agape, beckoning to Eli to enter.

The mist called to him again, and Eli made the sign of the cross, then crawled over the threshold into darkness. Behind him, the vapor lapped at the entry's deck just as the massive door creaked on its hinges to bar its entry, locking it out. The light flickered once before falling into darkness, and deep within the bowels of its massive walls, a monk's scream was suddenly silenced.

The Sullivan House was content… for now.

ONE

AUTUMN CAME EARLY THE YEAR Patrick was exon-
erated. Perhaps its timing at the end of a dark
southern summer was appropriate—a mirror of the
entire thirty-four years of his life. He turned hazel
eyes away from his reflection as he passed the last in
the line of courthouse windows and focused on the
broad staircase instead.

"My wife and daughter are dead." He pulled
uncomfortably at the lopsided tie draped around his
crumpled shirt.

"I know… I know," Gary said, one hand raised in
farewell to the blonde receptionist.

"But how…?"

"My greatest asset to you, as your attorney, is my
highly trained ability to be a good listener." Gary
brushed the lapel of his Ermenegildo Zegna suit and
offered Patrick a smile.

Patrick glanced at his attorney in disbelief. Atop
Gary's head, his waxed spikes had been tipped in

frosted auburn, a professional's touch, to be certain, and they stood out against his loosely cropped chestnut strands. It was obvious, the intention was to give him an air of reckless abandon within a perfect coif—a feat that had likely taken a full hour, at the least, to accomplish. Patrick's throat soured. He stared at Gary. The attorney's face was completely void of hair except for eyebrows plucked to perfection. Gary flashed his brilliant smile, completely oblivious to his client's knit brows and downturned mouth.

"The loss will never leave me," Patrick added in the hopes that, somehow, he would be heard this time.

Gary brushed the lapels of his suit, straightened the handkerchief hidden in the breast pocket, and opened the door to Kafe Java Coffee. The tiny coffee shop stood just feet from the edge of the Third District Courthouse.

"After you," he said with a sweeping motion of his hand. "That listening skill alone has brought us much success, as you can see. It's safe to say I've heard just about everything at this point." He followed Patrick into the coffee shop.

Deep, rich Columbian coffee hit Patrick's senses, and he drank in the scent for a moment. His tweed sports coat clashed with the rumpled blue shirt he wore. Patrick wished for warmer weather so he could abandon it somewhere. The contrast between client and attorney was too apparent and it felt to Patrick as if everyone seated within the tiny coffee shop noticed.

"Is there somewhere a little more private where we can talk?" Patrick shifted his weight and lowered his eyes.

"Oh, Pat, it's fine. I'm very comfortable here, and your case is over now, so there's no need to worry about anyone hearing anything too significant going forward." Gary flashed his grin and stepped up to the counter.

Nothing significant to anyone but me, Patrick thought. *What happened to client confidentiality, anyway?*

"Isn't that a problem with privacy and…?"

"Hello, darlin'," Gary stepped up to the bar and grasped a pretty brunette's hand.

"Hi, Gary." She offered her sweetest, dimpled smile.

There was little Patrick could do but join them at the bar and watch the barista carry on with his attorney. Behind the counter, the galley buzzed with activity. None of the workers looked each other in the eye as they blended, steeped, and frappe'd the mind-boggling variety of coffee drinks listed on the wall overhead. Patrick glanced up at the chalkboard scribbled with Italian coffee names he couldn't pronounce.

"Two java lattes please," Gary said.

"I don't drink…" Patrick started as Gary waved him off.

Patrick's life had been like that—someone else had always stepped in to decide what he wanted and how the future should look. Only recently had he taken matters into his own hands. Fate would be shaped by the way he wanted it from now on—or, at least, after coffee.

His wife had objected to everything at first, but quickly grew silent on each subject they had discussed, particularly recently, when Patrick insisted that "things change." Fortunately, his daughter was too little to offer any input and had silently gone along with her father's plans. All in all, it had worked out until the day law enforcement arrived on his doorstep and slapped handcuffs on his wrists.

The barista glanced at him briefly, then asked, "And for you, sir? What can I get you?"

"I'm with him," Patrick mumbled and pointed to the Ermenegildo Zegna suit that had made its way to an open table.

"Oh, okay then," she said and smiled. "He covered it."

Patrick dropped his gaze to the counter. While he didn't want to come across as a needy dolt, he knew that's what she was thinking. He said the only thing that came to mind.

"Your calendar is wrong." He nodded to a stationary block of jokes that covered the surface of a peel-away calendar.

"Uh-huh," she said and turned her focus to the woman who stood behind him in line. Patrick heard her dismissal loud and clear, so he quickly moved to where Gary sat. Without looking up, the attorney snapped open a black, eel-skin briefcase. Taking the only other available seat, Patrick sat down and folded his hands in front of him.

"Glad you're back, Pat. We've a few things to complete."

"They don't even know what date it is today," Patrick said as he felt his last shreds of control slipping away.

"It doesn't matter." Gary rifled through stacks of papers. "Now, if I could just get you to sign a few of these…"

He was cut off by his name being broadcasted from the counter. Just then, a long-legged blonde with a waist the size of most men's thighs and a chest to rival Dolly Parton's stepped between their table and the waiting drinks. Tight cutoffs, snipped to cup her ample derrière, offered a preview of her firm, rosy ass as she bent over to inspect the names scrolled over the waiting coffee cups.

"Eh, grab those, will you?" Gary asked and leaned back, eyes glued to her young, firm butt.

Patrick turned around in his chair just in time to see a wicked smile pass between his attorney and girl. Gary followed up with a quick wink that put color into her sun-kissed cheeks.

"Excuse me," Patrick interrupted. She tossed him a glance and stepped away, which broke Gary's eye contact. "I need to get past you to get our…"

"No worries," she said and tossed another grin to the guy in the designer suit, then turned with coffee in hand and made her way to another table. Patrick stepped around her, and within seconds, returned with a cup of steaming java in each hand and placed one in front of Gary.

"How old is she? Maybe seventeen?" he said as he resumed his seat.

"Who?"

"That girl there." Patrick glanced at her, then back to Gary. "Never mind. What papers do I need to sign? I thought we were finished."

"Just final stuff. Mostly signatures to close our professional association and your account." Gary shoved a bound bundle of papers forward, then set a gilded pen on top, smiled, and waited for the signature as he sipped coffee.

"I never thought I'd be in this predicament," Patrick muttered and picked up the pen. He made a show of scanning each page, but he never really looked at the words—it wouldn't matter, anyway. He'd still be forced to sign them.

"Like I said, I've seen it all," Gary interjected, and his stare darted to a point behind Patrick. "You know what I mean."

"Well, I'm trying…" Patrick trailed off, distracted by a paragraph that caught his attention.

"This is your chance to start fresh, Pat. Pick up and move on." Another grin flashed—one that Patrick saw without having to look up. He wasn't sure if Gary was even smiling at him.

"It's destroyed my life, my reputation, Gary!"

That snapped the attorney's attention back to the papers. He cocked his head and tapped a vacant line with his finger. "I do it for a living. It's my job to set people free. Today is your day, Pat."

Patrick scribbled his signature on the last line, then looked up into the attorney's face. "Gary, I have nothing. I've lost everything."

A short series of pats on one shoulder met his pleading looks. Gary's focus strayed back to the barista. "I know, buddy, I know. But maybe now you can leave everything behind and find a new place, get away from here, start over."

"Yeah, maybe."

"Good. Okay, well, we're done here." With a sweep, Gary reloaded the briefcase with the signed forms and tucked it snugly under his arm while clutching his coffee up in his other hand. Both men stood and made a motion toward the exit.

"Get that, will you, Pat?" Gary said, nodding to the door. Patrick pushed it open, then held it for his attorney and three joggers, who made their way inside with a simple, "Thanks." Patrick trotted behind Gary as he carefully balanced his coffee and caught up with Gary's long strides.

"What you're suggesting might be difficult for me."

"Exactly. This city is too small. People know your name here. Go somewhere new. It's a big world out there, Patrick." His eyes shifted to the parking structure on their right.

"Maybe that's a good idea."

"Of course it is." Gary turned for the stairs. "Okay, then. I've got to run. They need me back in the courtroom this afternoon."

"Yeah, okay… well, thanks."

Patrick watched him go. Mercifully, he didn't have to follow the legal defender any longer.

"Just doin' my job, Pat."

"Right, yeah, thanks… thanks, a lot, Gary." His attorney was too far away to hear. Suddenly, Gary spun on his heels and stared at him. Perhaps the lawyer had actually been within earshot, after all.

TWO

Amber and sienna light danced over the roof of Patrick's silver hatchback. He glanced at the sunset briefly before reaching for the handle on the driver's side. Jammed into the narrow space between the lever and the door rested a wadded-up real estate flyer. Patrick cursed and snatched it up. The thick ink felt sticky between his fingertips and left a stain on his skin. He cursed again and scanned the sidewalk for a trashcan.

"I'm so sick and tired of people trying to sell me shit!"

He glanced down again at the flyer in his hand. Across the top, in bold black letters, the words *Dream Home* caught his attention. *Gary suggested a new start.* The thought found its uninvited way into his head, but Patrick chose not to dismiss it just yet. *Maybe this is it… a little serendipitous nugget that's come my way.* He chuckled at the idea and folded the flyer in half, then slapped it against the open palm of one hand. Without another thought, he climbed into the driver's seat and started his car.

The drive through town was relatively short. Fortunately, Savannah offered a lot in the way of history and scenery. Some of the most fascinating sites were located off the main road, which provided an excuse to take the heavily wooded side roads now and then.

Today was a day that required a side trip. Patrick couldn't just go home—there really wasn't any home to go to, anyway. A one-bedroom loft above Uncle Jack's living room wasn't Patrick's idea of "home sweet home," but he didn't have much choice, under the circumstances.

Patrick made the unmarked right turn down the forgotten cobblestone road that led to the edge of the city. His Outback could handle the bumps for a while until the paved part of the road reappeared further on, closer to the water. He'd been down the road before and was amazed at the overgrowth and neglect. It was just what Patrick needed. Solitude and the chance to be forgotten for a while—to disappear without consequence. It was very inviting. He hoped the road had not been rediscovered since the last time he'd visited this part of Georgia. More than likely, there were others who had passed this way. Perhaps they, too, were looking for obscurity.

"Sweet oblivion." Patrick glanced at the rolled up flyer discarded on the passenger seat. "A new start in nowheresville."

Without warning, she was there.

"What the hell!" Patrick shouted and hit the brakes. The rear tires skidded against the gravel and spun to the left. His fist pounded the horn.

She wore a delicate blue and yellow flowered sundress that glistened in the scattered rays of light filtering in shards through the dense trees overhead. Sheer fabric fluttered as the breeze caught and held it for a moment. Her legs showed through the skirt as she meandered across the road only feet from the front of his car. Long trails of chestnut hair cascaded in waves to her waist. A single blue ribbon was tied in the back to hold whatever wisps she'd drawn back from her temple. Ahead of her was a stroller, and in it… a child.

Patrick honked again, but her pace never picked up. It did not slack, either. He watched with fascination as the woman glided past, unconcerned for her safety or the welfare of her child—or so it seemed. He pushed down on the steering wheel, blasting the horn at her. The woman still did not react.

Something caught his attention. A tendril of hair blew away from her face, exposing the gentle curves of her chin and high cheekbones. She turned her head and glanced at the sun—or perhaps at the source of the breeze, it was difficult to say. But her eyes were vacant and stared at something Patrick couldn't see. She smiled, and a chill ran down his spine.

His eyes darted to the visor on the passenger side. The mirror was dusty from disuse and the visor untouched. He pulled it down and a photo fell onto the seat next to the flyer.

"No! Can't be."

Patrick picked up the photo and stared down at it with trembling fingers, shaking the glossy image. His eyes darted back up to the woman who had stopped moving, her eyes staring at something in the distance. Patrick began to shiver. Slowly, he lifted the photo to eye level and glanced at it again. His gaze moved from the woman and back to the photo. There was no question. The woman was his dead wife, and the child, his daughter.

"No!" Patrick screamed and dropped the photo. Horror washed over him as he thought about approaching her. She still did not see him. "Annie," he whispered. He grabbed hold of the door handle, but froze. "Get out of the car, Patrick!"

Instead, Patrick sat there, staring at her—staring at the child.

What the hell do I do now? This can't be happening. It isn't possible. Thoughts assailed him and he threw both hands over his ears to stop them. The photo! He'd dropped the picture. It would be his only proof that this woman was his wife—alive! But that couldn't be. He'd watched as her body was lowered into the ground only a month ago. He had to speak with this woman—find out who she was. At least, if he were wrong, he would have a valid excuse for the mistake in identity. Perhaps the woman wouldn't think him a fool, after all, not if he showed her the photo. Perhaps…

He leaned over the seat and rummaged along the floorboards and underneath the seat. Nothing. Turning to get a better angle, he bent to the passenger door and leaned across the seat. A white corner stuck up from underneath the seat between the door and seatbelt carrier. He fumbled clumsily but could not reach it. Shifting to his knees, he reached across the seat once more and gripped the glossy edge, gently pulling it free. He lifted it up again and stared at it, then turned his head to glance out the windshield at the woman.

He saw nothing but the road.

THREE

"I'M LOSING MY MIND."

Patrick locked his hatchback, then turned the key that was still in the ignition. The sick sound of gears grinding against one another reminded him that the engine was already running.

"Shit! I'm totally losing it!" He popped the car into drive, then checked the road again, looking from one side to the other. "Where is she?" He scanned for the woman—his wife—but found nothing. "A ghost," he whispered to no one. His voice sounded rattled, and the tremble of his fingers confirmed it. *That was just weird!*

Ahead, the road curved and descended deeper into the woods lining the forgotten road to Bay Street. He'd been there before and knew the area somewhat. Still, his gut warned him to be cautious with a surreal uneasiness accompanying it. He decided to pay attention.

Not far into the turn, the wind began to pick up. Leaves and kindling blew in random gusts that kicked up dust from the road. Patrick shifted in his seat and flipped on the radio. Only one station played, and it was laced with static. Elevator music from the late '60s was discharged now and then, scratchy and distant-sounding. Still, it was better than nothing, so he left the channel alone.

He maneuvered the Outback around an S-curve, and the canopy began to open up. Sunlight blinked in and out of the treetops as he accelerated. Buddy Guy began to play the blues from another station that clicked in as the car found a clearing.

"'Bout time." Patrick repositioned himself in the seat. He sighed and tilted his head to one side, popping the bones along his spine. It always felt better when he did that. In the past, his wife would walk their daughter down his back—her tiny feet doing the work of his chiropractor.

"Sarah." He felt the tears well up behind his eyes, but quickly blinked and shook his head to scatter those thoughts. The toddler's memory began to fade, replaced by the image of the woman with the stroller. He glanced down at the glossy photo. It lay still in spite of the bumpy road. Patrick picked it up carefully by the corner so as not to touch its surface. He wasn't sure if this was because he didn't want to disturb the photo's gloss…or the images captured upon it. They had seemed to come alive on the isolated road not too far back, and he didn't want to repeat the delusion. If touching the photo disturbed the dead, he would certainly keep physical contact to the minimum.

"It's been a long day, Pat, ol' boy. You just imagined things back there." Patrick mimicked his father's Irish brogue and tossed the photo into the glove compartment.

As he navigated another curve, he spotted the water and breathed a little easier as the road swung down toward the ocean. In just moments, he would be able to see the Atlantic—and the waterfront shops that lined the river inlet. Screven Point supported only a few local businesses, but there would be people milling around and a place to get tanked if needed.

He turned again, and suddenly, the air grew dark, dusty, and filled with debris. He looked to its source and watched as a sand-spout twisted inward on itself. Branches and rocks the sizes of watermelons were pulled into its tunnel as it cavorted toward the road. Uncle Jack had called these "*Num*"—folklore he'd learned while on a service mission in Africa.

"How did Jack say it?" Patrick thought hard, trying to remember what his uncle used to say when he saw a dust devil on the road. *Where the Num flies, so goes the demon. It takes the body of one drawn to self-destruction, a soul who seeks release from his painful life.* The memory hit him like a thunderbolt. "Ridiculous!"

Reciting the warning again, Patrick waited, looking for any sign of truth to the African lore. "It is because of their evil nature—deceptively small, but equally as dangerous as a full-sized tornado." Patrick recited his uncle's saying and stopped the car, but kept the engine running. Better to wait it out and let the thing pass than to try to outrun it.

"*Num.*" Patrick repeated as if calling it by name would change its path. Instead, the twister seemed to pause—hesitating on the verge of destruction, or possibly, to seek out its prey—then suddenly shifted direction.

The funnel headed straight for Patrick.

He gunned the engine and flipped the car into reverse, kicking up dust and debris as he peeled out. Chances were that the car wouldn't escape damage, but he hit the accelerator anyway. The car backed down the street just as trees cracked and branches fell where he'd been only moments ago. Great gusts of wind swirled just ahead and slapped angry bursts of wind against the driver's side. Spastically, the Outback rocked, threatening to be tossed onto its side, but remained in place. Patrick stopped, put on the parking break, and waited.

The twister moved faster, seeking him out, or so it seemed. Its long spout—an elongated nose that swept from side-to-side—sniffed out the place where Patrick had been. It paused on the road just ahead of him. Patrick turned off the car and crouched down in the seat, hiding from the entity driving the twister. He held his breath and waited silently for the *Num* to travel again. If he moved, it would surely find him—somehow he knew this to be true, though reason suggested otherwise.

It darted to the right, searching the ground the way a bloodhound sniffs a trail. Patrick stopped breathing—perhaps the movement of his chest would give away his whereabouts. If he could just still his racing heart, all would be well. But that would mean death. Perhaps that was the only way to disappear from the entity hunting him. Perhaps death was the only answer.

Patrick shuddered and the *Num* lifted. It turned to the far side of the road and began to push through the underbrush. Debris carried from town flew as the wind picked up. Papers, bottles, and trash all swirled on the periphery of the twister, crashing angrily into the metal frame of the car shielding Patrick. He was thankful for that—the protection of a steel frame with shatterproof windows and locked doors.

Without warning, the *Num* shifted again, and with it, the wind changed direction, lessening its force. Patrick could hear its whine slowly fading into the distant woods as the twister moved farther away. He sat up and looked over the dash and through the windshield. His entire view of the road was obliterated. He blinked and realized the windshield was covered by something plastered onto it from the wind—some kind of paper or flyer stuck to his windshield. He tried the wipers, but they rolled over it.

"This is unbelievable!" Patrick said to himself.

The wind had died down enough for him to open his door. Prying it ajar a crack, he set one foot on the ground and waited. The *Num* did not respond—apparently seeking prey elsewhere. He sighed and opened his door, then stepped out to retrieve the flyer from the windshield.

"I can't believe this day. First court, then that hallucination—or whatever it was, on the road back there—and now this!"

He stopped mid-sentence and stared down at the flyer in his hands. Bold letters were scrolled across the top: *Dream Home*. He dropped the flyer and shot a look at the exact same flysheet lying on the seat of his car. Something was trying to connect with him.

FOUR

"This came for you."

Patrick had never seen the man behind the counter before. Steel gray eyes peered through shaggy eyebrows speckled with spidery strands of black hair protruding randomly from them. His lips pulled tight across yellowed teeth when he smiled, a sure sign that the gentleman had poured cheap whiskey and tobacco into his body for years—longer than Patrick had been alive, most likely. Bony prominences jutted out in various places beneath the oversized shirt that hung from his shoulders. Patrick guessed the shirt had once fit well.

"I'm sorry. I didn't get your name." The lines of Patrick's forehead deepened.

"I didn't give it to you yet." The old man stuck a bony hand across the glass counter that served as a display case. "Name's Wilkins."

Patrick shook the pale, bony hand. Beneath the thin layer of skin, he could feel the metacarpals and sinews of the old man's hand, ice cold and uninviting.

Outstretched in the other skeletal hand, Wilkins held cardstock that had been folded and sealed with a crimson wax stamp. With tenuous fingers, Patrick accepted it and turned it over to discover his name scrolled in elegant calligraphic handwriting. It appeared to have been written with a quill and ink.

Patrick M. Conner

"How did anyone know I would be here? I mean, I only just decided to turn into town a few minutes ago when I was driving…" Patrick broke off and stared at the old man, who only shrugged his shoulders.

"Dunno. It was left in the mail drop this morning when I got here." Wilkins eyes never left Patrick's face.

Patrick glanced behind at the mail slot set in the wall. To the left, the glass door displayed a blue plastic *Open* sign. His eyes travelled to a hat rack on one side. On nearly every hook, an artifact of some sort was hung. Most were vintage hats, canes, and scarves. Above these, a leather water pouch, timeworn and stained, was displayed.

"It's called a 'zahato,' and it's made of goatskin, carried by the Basque shepherds in the early 1800s," Wilkins said. "Nearly everything in here is from the eighteenth century, or earlier."

Patrick's gaze traveled along the interior of the shop. Every nook and cranny was stuffed with odd items and rare finds forgotten by those who once treasured them—most of the original owners were likely dead by now.

"What is this place?"

"Antiquities. I own the store." Wilkins paused. "Aren't you going to read the note?"

"Oh!" Patrick glanced down at the paper clutched in his fingers. "I almost forgot. I still don't understand how anyone knew I was going to be here."

"That your name?" Wilkins' eyes flashed as if they hid the answer behind them.

"Yes, it is, in fact." Patrick broke the wax seal. "This is so strange. No one in this town knows me... or, at least, I don't know anyone. That's why I chose this place."

"Seems like this place chose you." Wilkins let lose a wheezy laugh, sending chills down Patrick's spine.

"It would seem so." Patrick glanced down at the message written in the same meticulous handwriting.

The honour of your presence is requested as a guest of the Sullivan House.

"Who sent this?" Patrick heard the strain in his own voice that matched a knot taking root in his gut. "Who knows I'm here?"

He slowly made his way to one end of the store. It seemed to go on forever—another doorway led into a second building stacked to the ceiling with antique furniture and statues. Outside its windows, fountains and gargoyles stared back with dry, peeling faces.

"Hell if I know." Wilkins' voice carried from the front of the store. "Did you want to see the stuff in here? I can show you the place, if you're interested."

Patrick marched back into the main building and slapped the invitation down on the counter. "I want to know who sent this!"

"Perhaps you'd best go up to the Sullivan House and find out there. It's for sale, you know."

"For sale?" Patrick shifted his stance and retrieved the invitation. He stared down at it and sighed. "A real estate invitation. That's probably what this is. Promo stuff. But how did they know I would be here?"

The old man who shrugged again.

"I think I'd like to see this Sullivan House, after all. I'm in the market for a place. Maybe this is fate playing its hand."

"Maybe." Wilkins grabbed his jacket from off the coat rack. The old man flipped the *Open* sign to *Closed* and turned a key in the lock. Then faced Patrick. "You can follow me up there, if you're interested."

"So how come you know so much about this Sullivan House anyway?"

Wilkins stretched his thin lips over his yellowed teeth and his eyes flashed again.

"Because," Wilkins paused. "…I know who possesses it."

FIVE

Three months earlier—Savannah, GA

TINY CRACKS IN THE TIGHTLY drawn shade glistened with dust motes that fell in slow motion from somewhere overhead. His bleary eyes stared straight ahead, barely able to focus on the sparkles as they flitted across each beam of light. A single tear ran down his wrinkled cheek.

"I'm busy. You're just going to have to wait a minute." The voice came from the next room.

"I need you," he whispered.

She never came. The pain in his heart grew in comparison to the one that spread across his chest. He lifted a trembling hand and placed it there—across the place where the dull ache weighed heavily—experiencing the torture of a failing heart that no longer wanted to beat. *She's abandoned you for something else.* The thought tore at his chest again and another tear fell.

"You're so demanding!" Her voice was a whisper. "I can't do this anymore."

Using her teeth, she pulled the tourniquet a bit tighter over her bony bicep in hopes a vein would show itself. Track marks lined her forearms down to her fingers. She glanced at her legs, but they weren't any better—they had been used too many times, as well. She curled her fingers into a fist and pumped them opened and closed a few times with her eyes glued to the crease in her arm. Worming its way from deep beneath her skin, the telltale blue sign of a vein began to surface. She smiled.

"Help me!" he called out again from the other room, but she ignored him.

This was too important, and he couldn't pull her away from it, not now. Lifting the syringe from its resting place on the table, she leveled the bevel of the needle alongside the pale blue outline and pierced the skin. The needle slipped in easily—she barely felt it anymore—the irritation of his incessant cries disappearing as quickly as the prick of the hypodermic.

"Please." His voice was softer, but still irritated her—like fingernails on a chalkboard.

"Shut up!" she yelled and withdrew the needle from her arm. The tourniquet lay discarded, no longer needed as her vein fed her the cooked crystal she had just injected. She closed her eyes. "Just… shut up!"

"I… someone… please…"

His voice was softer now—easier to ignore. Soon she would no longer hear it. The drug would take her away from this place, away from him, away from the nightmare that had become her life. She never asked for this—never asked to be his caregiver—or his daughter.

The old man fell silent. His hand had dropped from his chest and lay limp against the bed sheets. His eyes were wide, unblinking, and stared at the dust motes that fell through the sun's rays lying against his face. His broken heart had finally succumbed, quivered, and stopped. Its final beat had gone unnoticed. The only person in his life had chosen to let him die.

She glanced one last time at the room. He was asleep, apparently. *Finally! Maybe I'll have a moment's reprieve.* She felt the drug's "high" hit and longed for a time without having to think about him. *Only a few moments left to do this.*

Turning toward the front door, she noticed that his wallet lay forgotten atop the abandoned bookcase. *He'll never know the difference.* The thought curled the corner of her lips as she emptied it of the bills and credit cards tucked neatly inside. *He'll never know.* It played in her drugged mind over and over again. She glanced over her shoulder at the old man and decided there was one last thing to do.

The smell of a sick room accosted her senses, so she held her breath. Against the sheets, his hand lay limp, cold, and unresponsive. A single gold band encircled the fourth finger of his left hand. *He'll never know the difference.* She exhaled, quickly pinched the gold between her fingers, and slipped the ring off.

Without looking back, she walked out without closing the door.

Recompense will find you as death has quietly found him. The thought did not come from her, although she heard it.

SIX

Present day—Savannah, GA

LOOMING COLUMNS, ROOTED CENTURIES AGO, rose from the ground, with grotesques the size of live gorillas glaring down from stone pillars lining both sides of an iron gate. Vines clung fearfully to each pillar as the estate's entrance fed life to them. Withered leaves decomposed to a crisp brown where they hung. Something lived within the bulwark that did not grow from nature.

Patrick's eyes followed the stone columns to the top and rested on the face of the grotesque. Its eyes were black, shiny, and looking back at him. *It stares at me.* He shivered and returned his gaze to the gravel road that stretched ahead under dense tree cover. Wilkins' truck had already moved ahead, passing quickly through the columns.

For some reason, the grotesques did not stare at Wilkins.

The sunlight glistened through the canopy, giving off the same eerie feeling that Patrick had experienced earlier that day when he drove under a similar patch of treetops. He wondered if this was unusual. Did all of Savannah have dark roads lined with dripping moss on woodland trees. They should be sentries but felt more like monsters with snaking fingers reaching to grab anything human that passed by. *Ridiculous! Your imagination is getting the best of you, Pat. Snap out of it!*

Wilkins' red truck stood out against the dark, a single drop of crimson that followed the main artery leading to the heart of the property.

"No one ever drives this way, apparently. Shitty dirt road," Patrick cursed as a rock hit the windshield. "This day stinks!" He wondered if this was not a coincidence, as well.

Suddenly, the trees parted, and a vast expanse opened into what had once been a majestic estate. A stone barrier followed the perimeter and disappeared into the deeper brush that buried it along with its history. To one side, a small, fenced plot rested quietly underneath another line of dripping willow trees—its center stippled with headstones that marked the beds for the dead who lay there. Patrick shuddered again.

He pulled the Outback to a halt at the top of a curved driveway and stepped out. A miscreation of stone and wood stared down at him—an ancient manor house whose spires towered above the lush canopy. Through blackened windows, its unblinking eyes—the soul of the Sullivan House—stared at him, dark and sinister… and alive.

Patrick stared in disbelief. How could a mansion with such archaic elegance call to him? His hands trembled.

"It's staring at me," Patrick whispered to no one.

Ahead, Wilkins had stepped out of his truck. He stood facing the house with a contented smile crossing his thin lips. Patrick wondered how the old man could be so calm—especially with the house looking down at him. *It's in your head, Pat.* The thought came uninvited. *Aftereffects of a long day that began in court. Relax, buddy.* He doubted he would.

To one side, a woman sat on the edge of the massive front porch entry. Her jeans and t-shirt hung over emaciated arms, and her hair looked as if it hadn't seen a brush in years. She glanced at Patrick with sallow eyes and followed him as he closed the car door. He lifted a hand to wave out of courtesy, then thought better of it. Her look was vacant, empty of any ability to respond.

"What's with her?" Patrick said in low tones, stepping up alongside Wilkins.

"She's the newest resident of Sullivan House." Wilkins smiled at this. He sounded as if it were an everyday occurrence. "Her father was found dead in his bed just three months ago. She's an addict, and rumors around town say that she abandoned him. She probably could have saved him if she'd stayed put. They didn't find the body for nearly two weeks. His dog…"

"Was she his caregiver?" Patrick cut him off, unable to hear more and unwilling take his eyes from the ghoulish figure sitting on the porch.

"Yes. I mean, that's what family is for, right? To care for one another." Wilkins looked at Patrick from the corner of his eye. Then, turning back to the house, he continued, "They say he called out for her… called out for help, and she ignored him, left him to die alone. They say there were needles on the table and an empty wallet left on a bookcase near the door. They say…"

"I got it," Patrick cut him off again. "So what's the deal with this house? It's freezing here… gives me the creeps."

"That's just because it's in the shadows." Wilkins waved to the trees. "The house is very old—more than three centuries. It's the oldest intact structure in Savannah. It's got character and history and… well, let me show you." Wilkins stepped forward but Patrick stayed put.

"Look, I've had second thoughts. I think I'll just go back to town and find a nice hotel to stay in. This place… there's something wrong with it. Besides, there are other people who…" He broke off. "Why *is* she here, anyway?"

Wilkins grinned, and his thin lips blanched, but he made no attempt to stop Patrick from his sudden retreat. The sun moved behind a cloud to cast deeper shadows over the entire estate of the Sullivan House. Shrouded in obscurity, Wilkins had the appearance of a ghost—as did the woman. Patrick backed toward his car. He could feel the house watching him as he moved.

"The Sullivan House is a place of shelter. It houses those who have—issues, let's call them. It's for those who need help… help to face their own circumstances."

"It doesn't feel like a place to help anyone."

"Consider the house a place of refuge for souls who cannot be amongst those with full lives—a place for recompense, as it were."

"I don't understand," Patrick said, pausing at the door to his car.

Wilkins moved a hand toward the woman. "She is unable to function in society, so she is here. It's very simple, Patrick."

"Like a halfway house?"

"I suppose that's one way to look at it." Wilkins clenched his hands together and dropped them in front of him. He remained where he was, at the precipice of the massive stairwell that led to the front entry.

"Then why me? Why did someone invite me to the house?" Patrick retrieved the invitation and waved it over his head. "I don't need a halfway house. I don't need to be out of society."

Wilkins's face froze with pale lips still stretched into the grin. "You are looking for lodging, correct?"

"Well, yeah," Patrick admitted and glanced down at the paper clutched between his fingers.

"You're looking to get away, to find a new start?"

"Yes."

"Perhaps that's all it is. It knows what you need and stands ready to take you in." Wilkins' voice sounded almost wistful as he gazed up at the spires lining the house. A pair of grotesques seemed to nod at him from their perches.

Patrick's gaze followed, and he shuddered again. Something wasn't right about the place. He felt it—cold, predatory. He forced his gaze away from the structure and stared at Wilkins.

"How do you know so much about what I want?"

"I know only what you've told me, and what's on the invitation in your hand there."

Patrick held it up. "Who sent this? Who knows what I need better than me, huh?" Patrick snapped.

Wilkins eyed Patrick coldly, and the woman mirrored him. His pale lips parted as he whispered just three words: "The Sullivan House."

SEVEN

THE NEON SIGN FLICKERED, BEGGING forlorn customers to come inside and pay a visit. Occasionally, the light would spasm and go dark, only to blink *Open* in bright red again. Patrick pulled his Outback into the closest parking space and turned off the engine, staring up at the illuminated sign. Surely, it was more inviting than the creepy old house down the road. It beckoned to him, too, only in a good way. He needed a drink, and needed it badly.

A short walk to the entry only confirmed it—his legs trembled nearly as fiercely as his hands. *Damn crazy old man!* Patrick's thoughts screamed inside his head. *Damn freakin' house!* He pushed against a mahogany carved door and caught sight of letters that read: *Tondee's Pub House.*

It was painted on sea wood. Patrick waited a moment for his eyes to focus in the dim light, then strolled to a long, padded counter and sat on an empty stool at the bar.

"Whiskey."

The bartender nodded and turned his back on Patrick. Facing a line of half-empty bottles, he pretended to be preoccupied. From the full-length mirror, Patrick could see the man's eyes on him and dropped his gaze to study a matchbook that had been tossed next to a dirty ashtray on the counter.

"Visiting here?" the bartender said, setting down a glass filled with ice cubes and clear liquid.

"Yeah." Patrick lifted the glass to his lips. "Thanks." He paused, tipped the glass in salute to the bartender, and then took a mouthful. It burned his throat as he swallowed, but it felt better than the angst blistering his gut. *A warning, to be certain. Something's wrong with that old man, Wilkins, and his nasty, evil house.* Patrick took another mouthful of the whiskey and swallowed the thought.

"Why are you here?"

"Just passing through." Patrick shot a look at the bartender. Obviously, the man had seen that look before, because he did not react. He only nodded.

"Okay."

"I… uh… say, what do you know of that place they call the Sullivan House?" Patrick casually sipped his drink, eyes on the bartender.

"I know I wouldn't go in there." The bartender glanced briefly at Patrick, then turned away again.

Apparently, the Sullivan House wasn't a popular topic with him—something Patrick guessed he'd been asked about before. Whatever he might say, Patrick knew the man wasn't going to tell him everything.

"It's filled with treasure."

A voice, deep and raspy, spoke from the far end of the bar. Patrick turned to see a pair of eyes the color of cut sea glass buried in tight folds of leathery skin. Spittle pooled in the corner of the old man's mouth. He grinned, exposing yellowed teeth.

"What do you mean?" Patrick picked up his drink and walked toward the salty dog. Taking a seat next to him, Patrick looked from the bartender to the old man's leathery face. "What do you mean, 'It's filled with treasure?'"

"This here's Mickey," the bartender interjected. He picked up a just-washed glass and began wiping it with a dirty bar towel.

"Mickey," Patrick said and nodded. "So, tell me what you know about the Sullivan House."

Mickey stared at Patrick and his grin softened as the lines deepened on his forehead. "Another, Frank," Mickey wheezed. Without pause, the bartender poured another shot into Mickey's glass.

"Mickey's been around here the longest. He knows more than anyone, I suspect," Frank added as he picked up another washed glass and began to wipe it dry with the same dirty towel.

Patrick waited.

"No one's ever gone in there that's come out again." Mickey's voice sent chills down Patrick's already prickling spine.

"What do you mean?"

Frank picked up another glass. "There's money bein' made in there, Mick. Somebody comes out sometimes."

Mickey's eyes shifted to the bartender. "No one alive."

"What are you saying?" Patrick blurted out, but Mickey kept his steady gaze on Frank, whose hands had suddenly stopped moving.

"Aye, payin' to get in. Maybe that's the secret o' the Sullivan House," Mickey said, shifting his gaze back to Patrick.

"What's this about treasure?" Patrick asked again. "I don't think there's any treasure left anywhere that hasn't already been discovered." He forced down the anticipation in his voice.

"I'd give anything for what's buried up there," Mickey said and took another shot from his glass.

"Up there?"

"Up there on the hill… where the Sullivan House rests," Frank added.

"You talk as if it's dead. 'Buried' and 'rests on a hill?'" Patrick knocked back his drink. "What's that about? A house like that wouldn't hold any 'buried treasure' in it. Too active. Too many people there. The house looks like it kicked the bucket a while ago."

"It's far from dead, mate," Mickey said, his voice barely a whisper.

"You mean the house is alive? Gimme a break," Patrick said. "I don't believe in…" He shivered and motioned for another whiskey. Frank poured him another drink. Apparently eager to revisit talk of the Sullivan House with Mickey, he set the bottle down and leaned over the bar, eyes on Mickey.

"Aye," Mickey said. "The house lives—a breathin', soulless pile o' evil. Deep inside lay treasure taken from a monastery. It's cursed!"

"Ah, Mickey just likes to scare people," Frank said, slapping the bar counter with his towel. "Don't listen to his tall tales."

Patrick looked from Frank to Mickey. It was hard to know who to believe. Tall tales from seafarers were as common as mosquitoes on a Savannah summer day, but something about Mickey's story went against Patrick's better judgment. Mickey watched Patrick, and his eyes flashed, the same look that Patrick had seen in Wilkins' eyes earlier. Perhaps Mickey was just as crazy as Wilkins. Mickey grinned and his eyes gleamed.

"You know I'm tellin' you true."

"Cursed treasure? Monks? You're talking about a real, live haunted house? This is all craziness!" Patrick snapped and set down a twenty-dollar bill on the counter. "Thanks." Patrick looked at Frank and stood to leave. "And thanks for the stories, old man." He waved a hand as he made for the door.

"Be wary of those who would send you astray, Patrick. This is your chance to begin anew," Mickey replied.

By then, Patrick had reached the door. He paused with his hand hovering against the mahogany wood. *How does the old man know?* The thought brought chills.

"Yeah… thanks," Patrick said, and pushed the door open.

As he walked out, he heard the old man laugh— the same wheezy laugh that belonged to Wilkins.

EIGHT

THE DRIVE BACK TO SAVANNAH left Patrick a bit on edge—not that his encounter with Wilkins or strange old Mickey had put him at ease. If anything, the events of the day, beginning with the calendar block at the coffee shop, had been nothing but eerie. Patrick rounded a corner and half expected to see a ghost— perhaps the woman with her stroller again.

"Get a grip, Patrick," he said aloud, wondering if anyone else could hear him talk.

As he neared the canopy that blanketed the next leg of his drive, he stopped the car and glanced in both directions. Debris from the *Num* still cluttered the road, and while Patrick couldn't see evidence of the *Num's* twin, there was an uneasiness about these woods. The thought of driving back down a road that had nearly been his *location mortis* left him feeling unsettled.

The forked road left him two choices: take the road where he'd nearly been killed or, as the poem suggested, the one less travelled. Patrick decided to take a chance with fate and turned onto the rugged, untraveled fork. Just where it would take him, he had no idea, but he wasn't going to risk another African devil's *Num*—not twice in the same day.

The canopy grew thick and dense with each mile. Grateful for the four-wheel option, Patrick shifted and decided to take it slow. Occasionally, the sound of some creature would catch him off guard, making him jump.

"This is a freakin' nightmare," he said aloud, glancing up at the treetops.

As if it knew Patrick was staring upward, suddenly, out of nowhere, a massive owl swooped down at his car and aimed with massive talons at Patrick's eyes. Its claws scratched against the only barrier shielding Patrick. The windshield was left gouged as the owl scrabbled the glass, then lifted its grey, ghostly wings and disappeared again into the canopy.

Patrick hit the brakes. "What the hell was that?" he said, waiting for his heart to stop pounding. Sitting there for a moment longer, he stared into the dark, wooded expanse at an empty dirt road.

Breathe. The thought came to mind, and he took a deep, slow breath. Maybe that would slow his racing heart, but he doubted it. Patrick was scared. *Scared of what? An owl that you nearly ran over? Get a grip!*

He dropped his gaze to the radio knobs on the dashboard, but thought the better of it—static from a radio would just make this drive creepier than it already was. Dropping the Outback into gear, he readied for the drive and looked back to the road.

She was there.

Her face contorted against the window, and her voiceless, pleading gaze was locked on his. Blood smeared the front of her dress.

"No!" Patrick screamed.

Ahead, on the road, the stroller blocked his only access. Blood dripped from it onto the dirt as a tiny hand held tightly to a stuffed lion Patrick remembered was his daughter's birthday gift. He'd given it to her when she was only three.

"No! No! No!" he hollered again and threw the Outback into reverse.

The woman fell away from the window as the car skidded away from her.

Patrick.

He heard the whisper echo as if it was inside his head. Behind, the road was clear and sunlight poured through at the end of the canopy. That was his goal— the clearing and sunlight. He glanced back to the road in front and watched as the woman with her stroller slowly faded from view.

Patrick.

His foot hit the gas as he U-turned the car to face the light in the distance.

Patrick.

Out of habit, he glanced in the rearview mirror. She was there. Her tears bathed her blood-splattered face. His foot lurched on the gas pedal, sending his car into a rear skid that he quickly recovered from.

"Get away from me!" Patrick screeched.

Fog had begun to envelop the car, dampening the window with condensation, and he found it difficult to see. He flipped on the wipers but they did little to clear it. Quite by accident, he brushed the driver's side window with his sleeve, leaving a long streak that revealed the side woods. There was no fog outside—the mist that coated the Outback's windows was from the *inside*.

Patrick.

He looked to the passenger window and she was there—sitting in the passenger seat. Blood dripped onto the leather, and as she placed her hand on the window, leaving deep crimson streaks.

Patrick.

An aroma of rotting flesh filled the confines of the cab as she spoke, causing Patrick to gag. In slow motion, she reached toward him with a bloody hand.

"Get away from me, Sara!"

It was too late for him now… he'd said her name. She touched his arm and the flesh burned where it made contact.

"You're dead. *Dead!*" Patrick screamed at her.

Suddenly, the Outback emerged into light that illuminated the cab's interior. Patrick glanced at his arm, then back to the ghost. She was gone. Instantly, his windows cleared and he stared straight ahead at the fork in the road.

Patrick pulled the car to a halt and leaned back in his seat. "What the hell!… What…?" He couldn't breathe. "Who? Oh, shit! Not this road… not me!" His voice came in gasps as he stared straight ahead at the road. "Bad choice, Pat!" He tried to laugh, but it sounded more like a gasp. Rolling his window down just enough to allow the smell of pine to wash over his face, he sat, eyes closed, heart pounding. The hallucination was gone.

"Bad whiskey," he said, rationalizing a likely side effect from the forgotten pub. After a moment, he opened his eyes and dropped the Outback into gear. There was nowhere else to go except back the way he'd come. "You can spend a night in a small town for once," Patrick said, urging the Outback forward.

He took another deep breath and found that his heartbeat had slowed in time with his breathing. *Panic attack*, he told himself. *None of it was real*. And, to confirm it, he glanced at the seat next to him.

"See, no blood… nothing there," he said. Then he looked up at the window.

Streaked along the glass was a single handprint in crimson.

NINE

Dusk cloaked the coastline with a dank shroud, typical for autumn days found in a potter's field. Patrick had been less concerned about the evening's pall as he approached the road's fork than he was about what lay behind him. Neither exit from the tiny village left him a viable option in his mind, and the only way he could escape the nightmare of ghosts and demons was to drive straight back to Screven's Point.

Tondee's Pub House was still open. Faint yellow light illuminated the windows, contrasting with the flickering red *Open* sign that beckoned Patrick to return. *No way in hell*, he thought as he drove past, certain that Frank and old man Mickey would be in the same place he'd left them only an hour earlier.

"There has to be a hotel somewhere in this stinkin' town!"

Toward the end of the road, a green sign spelling out V-A-C-A-N-C-Y caught his eye. He cared little about its condition. The place could be rundown and filled with roaches, and it wouldn't matter at this point. In fact, he suspected the hotel *would* likely be a bug-infested, "One-Star Special" dive. He just wanted a place to sleep for the night. There would be no going back to Savannah, not now, and not in the dark.

"Gear up to sleep with the roaches tonight, Pat. You've earned it, apparently," he said and pulled into a gravel lot used for parking.

Only one other car sat in a vacant space in front of a painted red door with the number *9* in brass tacked onto it. Directly ahead, a tiny office sat with its door propped open—most likely to let in a breeze. The night had grown muggy, in spite of the sun's disappearance, and Patrick could see the vestiges of fog crawling up from the coastline.

"Hello?" he said as he stepped inside the bleak office. No one was around that he could see, and the counter that took up most of the interior's space was vacant of anything except a silver bell. Patrick tapped it once. "Hello? Is anyone here?"

He glanced through a small doorway behind the counter and saw a TV broadcasting grey static in front of an empty, oversized chair. Cigarette smoke hung in the air. He decided to look outside and stepped back onto the narrow walkway that lined the entire length of the single-story motel.

"Definitely a roach hotel," Patrick said under his breath.

"Excuse me?" The voice came from behind and startled Patrick enough to raise the hair on the back of his neck.

"I… I didn't see anyone inside. I'd like a room for the night," Patrick said, swallowing back the quiver in his voice.

"I see."

The woman was frail, although her voice sounded thinner than she looked. She stared at him with vacant eyes that suggested she'd seen too much in her sixty-plus years.

"The sign said there was a vacancy and I just…"

"Follow me," she said and turned back into the office. She slipped behind the counter and made a selection from the line of keys that dangled from a plaque on the wall. "Room 6." She handed the key to Patrick.

"Don't you want my credit card or something?" He took the key from her and noticed it looked old, fragile, and unused.

She stared at him for a moment, then pulled a book out from beneath the counter and opened it to the center. Lines filled with names written in handwriting that looked like those Patrick had seen scrolled across ancient documents covered the page. He scanned the names as he browsed for the next vacant line. Alongside each signature was a date—the last one written as June 6, 1842.

"I think your dates are off."

The woman glanced at the page, then back to Patrick.

"Is this correct?" he asked, pointing to the year. "1842? Really? This place wasn't even built then."

Again, the woman's eyes dropped to the page, but she said nothing. Shaking his head, Patrick entered his name on the next line. Then, setting the pen down, he forced a smile, offered his thanks, and walked out of the office.

Room Six had not been used in a long, long time. The smell was enough to drive Patrick back to the pub, but not foul enough to send him back into the forest. Flipping the wall switch, a single-bulbed lamp clicked to life. It flickered a bit, likely due to a sudden surge of electricity that had not run that course for so long. To one side, a solitary desk faced a blank wall that had a solitary painting hanging in a gilded frame—a landscape with hounds that ran ahead of three horses ridden by hunters in red frocks and black boots. In the middle of the only other wall, a double-sized bed rested. The burnt orange coverlet draped over it was nearly three inches too short on all sides, leaving a gap that revealed a bed frame made of bent aluminum.

This is going to be a long night, Patrick thought as he made his way to the bathroom. He washed his hands and was grateful the linen and chrome, though worn, was clean and the water hot. After depositing his belongings onto the luggage rack, he walked to the only window and cranked a handle. The dusty glass and hinges begged to remain in place, but after some urging, the wood frame gave way. Muggy, outside air poured into the confined space that would be Patrick's sleeping quarters for the night, bringing little relief to the stuffy room.

It was getting late and Patrick was hungry. He stood at the window and breathed in the sticky night air. Patrick decided to grab a bite to eat. *At least it will be a chance to look around town while this room airs out… hopefully.*

Interrupting his thoughts, scratchy white noise blasted from the bedside radio. Patrick jumped. *"What the hell?"*

He made his way to the clock and noticed the time illuminated in digital green. "Six minutes after six and oh-six seconds. That's nice."

He flipped off the radio and the room fell silent. Patrick let his eyes rest upon the object for a moment. Something unsettled him. *You're just jumpy from everything that's gone on today—weird day!* And then it struck him. The time still blazed in green, but the seconds had disappeared. "That's weird," he said and thumped the clock with his palm. Still no seconds appeared on the clock's face. He picked up the clock and looked at the bottom of it—nothing unusual.

"You just read six minutes after six and oh-six seconds," he said, speaking to the clock as if it could hear him. "I saw it! Slimy green, you piece of shit! Six-six-oh-six."

Patrick froze, dropping the clock to the floor. The realization of what he'd just said hit him like bricks. "Six-six-six," he whispered and backed away. "I gotta get out of here and clear my head." He grabbed the keys to his hatchback. "Time to eat and get away from this place, this freaking town!" He stepped out, locking the door to Room Six behind him.

TEN

"WHAT'S THAT OVER THERE?" PATRICK pointed through a window to an old building across the street. The waitress stopped and looked out the window.

"Oh, that," she said, filling his glass. "Forsythe Square. That's the Confederate Monument in the middle. It's been around since the 1870s. There's a Paris fountain too. Oh, and that's Chandler Oak." She nodded her head toward the window, as if Patrick would know what she was looking at. "That tree there is where crooks were hung. It's known as 'The Hangin' Tree.'"

"No, wait… like a gallows?"

She nodded and smiled. Something crashed in the kitchen and Patrick suddenly became acutely aware of the smells inside the diner—old grease and coffee.

"Is something wrong?"

"I… uh… 'character' is how they describe places like this. I guess that tree has character too?" He let loose a nervous chuckle and scanned the diner.

The place was relatively empty except for an older couple that hadn't spoken to each other during the entire time he'd been there. Once in a while, he'd catch a rogue glance his way, but the man would immediately drop his gaze as Patrick met it. This time, the woman sitting in the booth turned to gawk at him. It happened again as Patrick stared back. *Strange place.*

"Yessir," the waitress said, butting into Patrick's thoughts. "They used to bury the bodies there too. The street runs over the graves—mostly in the morgue tunnel that runs from the hospital to the park, over there." She leaned in closer as if to whisper, but the level of her voice remained the same. "They say it's haunted, you know."

"No, I didn't know." Patrick swallowed and glanced out the window again. "Actually, I was wondering about the building." He pointed again.

"Well, you should learn about some of the history in Savannah. It's one of the oldest, most haunted cities in the U. S. of A." She smiled proudly as if she'd just passed on a valuable piece of history to a foreigner. "Most of 'em were from the Yellow Fever."

"I'm sorry?"

"Yup. Yellow Fever—came in from the boats. Lots of people died. Kind of creepy, actually. There was exactly six hundred sixty-six people who died." She nodded and wrote in the air with a finger three numerals: 666. "That's the devil's number, ya know."

Patrick cleared his throat. "I'm sorry, can you tell me a little more about that place there?"

The ancient building looked worn, though not neglected. Its surface was wrapped with colonial trappings that peaked from the roof's leader. A crisply carved, white stone stairway rose up to meet a solid mahogany door that was overshadowed by a two-column portico at the entrance. Two lion statues stood like sentries at an ancient iron gate where trees flanked a thick, but well-mowed, lawn that pushed to the street. The entire estate was surrounded by a solid iron fence. Without question, the building was old and filled with stories of its own.

"Oh, that's Hedge Hall… the library," she replied, matter-of-factly. "Can I get you anything else?" She looked away from the window and started clearing the empty dishes from the table.

"Just the check, please. Do you know how late the library stays open?" he added as an afterthought and scraped the last vestiges of dark gravy from his plate with a chunk of bread just before he handed it to her. "Thanks."

"Welcome." Balancing the added plate on her forearm, she glanced out the window again. "The library closes officially at five, but sometimes it's open later… until nine, I believe. At least, that's when I see the lights go out over there. Wish we closed at nine, but no…" She trailed off as she made her way back to the kitchen.

Patrick dropped a twenty-dollar bill on the table and walked out. Eyes stared him down as he headed toward the couple and the exit just beyond.

"Best stay away, boy."

The voice was but a whisper as Patrick walked by. He let his eyes wander to the old man's face. His expression was blank, no emotion, as if he'd said nothing at all.

"I'm sorry. Did you say something to me?"

The old man squinted as he stared at Patrick, never blinking. "I'm warnin' you, is all. That place is bad. A vile house filled with a dark soul inside."

Patrick snorted. "The damn house isn't alive."

"Some say it is."

"Yeah, well, we'll see."

"It'll be too late by then."

Patrick shook his head and stepped outside. "Odd, some of the people here." He paused, inhaling deeply to clear his nostrils of the greasy smell that lingered from inside. Across from him, the library stood with a single row of windows illuminated on the main floor. "Still open, maybe… at least for another forty-five minutes, if I'm lucky."

Stepping onto the roadway, he glanced down the street. All traces of sunset had disappeared long ago under the high canopy overhead. Spanish moss dripped from most of the branches, giving an eerie, ominous feeling to the night.

He looked the other way. Nothing there—no headlights from oncoming cars, no pedestrians, not even small animals. The road was as empty as the night.

Darting across to a path that led through a small iron gate, Patrick guessed that the entrance had once been the hub of the city. Likely, this was not a library in its inception—or so Patrick surmised. In truth, the building had been used to house records of births, marriages, property deeds, and wills. "The Georgia Historical Society, a relic," the waitress had said.

It had also been used to confine the insane and those deemed unfit for society. Sensing the building's secret, Patrick paused to look around. A shudder ran along his spine. It felt as if someone was watching him. He looked at the gate.

"Stupid lions," he said and stepped up to the landing. Eyes made of stone seemed to follow him, though they remained focused forward. Taped to a window-pane, a tiny sign displayed the library hours.

Open until 5:00 PM.

"Interesting." Patrick pushed open the unlocked door. Iron hinges groaned, announcing his arrival, and the musty smell of old books and dried ink hit his nostrils. He took one last breath of outside air, then moved inside, allowing the door to close on its own behind.

Ahead, rows of books coated walls that rose nearly thirty feet overhead to a ceiling that was crisscrossed with beams the color of charcoal. Two rows of solid walnut tables lined the length of the cavernous room, filling in the space between the entrance and the farthest wall. Chairs the same shade as the ceiling beams were evenly spaced on every side of each table. Hung at an angle over floor-to-ceiling bookcases, portraits of scowling men and sour women stared down in disapproval.

Tacked on one wall, a sign read *Reading Room*. Patrick wondered whether a warm body had ever really sat to read in there, and guessed it had been a while, since most of the chairs were covered in dust. Obvious care had been taken to tuck each one deep beneath its designated table, where they remained, untouched.

"Hello?" Patrick called out. His only answer came from his own voice as it ricocheted within the rafters above. Lining the entire chamber, rows of shelving abruptly ended in a series of sharp turns, giving the library an appearance of a giant maze.

Patrick glanced down an opening in one of the bookcase walls. Another chamber awaited, dark and tomb-like. Taking long strides, he made his way deeper into the chamber and called out again. "Is anyone here?"

ELEVEN

PATRICK HEARD IT—AT ALMOST THE same time he had called out, something made its presence known. He turned to face it, a found himself staring at nothing but books and darkness.

Just then, the clicking of high-heeled footsteps sounded from one of the alcoves to Patrick's right. He looked to the sound but saw no one accompanying the noise. *Click-click-click.* He cocked his head and stared into a dark hallway but saw nothing. The sound continued and seemed to grow louder.

"Hello?" He swallowed, waiting in hopes that someone would materialize attached to the footsteps.

"How may I help you?"

The voice came from behind. Patrick spun around, jumping backward as he came face-to-face with a woman. Her hands were clasped in front and her pale blue eyes glinted a bit as she stared at him. He dropped his gaze to her feet and saw they were indeed dressed in black leather heels. "I heard you coming and I…"

She shifted her weight. "Yes, well, this is a very old building with unusual acoustics. Now, what may I do for you?"

"I'm looking for a book," he said, though the words sounded unnatural. "I mean, I'm looking for information that might be in a book." That sounded worse. Patrick cleared his throat and heard it echo in the rafters.

"What kind of information are you looking for?" The woman's voice was soft, wispy, soothing to his rattled nerves.

"I'm not sure, actually. A book or newspaper or journal… anything, really." Patrick fumbled with his keys. His attempt to sound nonchalant failed again.

"About what?"

"A house. The Sullivan House, to be precise."

"Oh." She stared at him for a moment and the glint faded from her eyes. "And what do you want to know about *that* house?"

Her tone unsettled him even further. Perhaps she was toying with him—perhaps this was the way people protected their history in the South. Patrick shuddered again. Young women didn't usually act so cryptic, and libraries didn't smell like a morgue, either.

"What is this place… really?" he asked.

"It's a library, sir."

"Patrick," he said and offered a hand. "Just call me Pat."

She smiled and took his hand. Her fingers felt frail and ice cold in his, and he wondered if he should offer his jacket. "Are you chilly?"

"Why, no…Patrick. Why?" She smiled and canted her head to one side as she looked at him with the same stony stare as the lions outside.

"Pat, please."

"I'm just fine, thank you. Why do you ask?"

"Never mind. I just thought that…" Patrick withdrew his hand and dropped it into his jacket pocket. "I just want some information about the history of the Sullivan House. Is there anything here on record?"

"In fact, you're in luck." She turned and started walking. "Follow me. There are some articles from news clippings on microfiche about the original inhabitants of the house. It's kept in the archives."

She began to walk toward a darkened alcove at the far end. Patrick paused only a moment before he thought better of being left behind, alone in the great chamber. He glanced overhead and the ceiling seemed to loom ominously. The beams crossed in patterns that looked like symbols warning him to move on.

"I would offer the computer as an option, but we don't have these records updated." She waved a hand at some unseen filing system. Patrick guessed they still used the old Card Catalog system. He'd never quite figured out how to use it as a kid in school and was grateful when books were logged online. Savannah seemed to be unconcerned with moving into modern times.

Another charming trait of the South. He smiled at the thought and realized he'd lagged behind again.

"Are you coming, Patrick?"

Jogging to keep up, he feigned interest in a globe set on a table nearby. "Oh, yes, just looking… uh, I didn't get your name." Patrick's voice echoed overhead once again.

She didn't respond, but, instead, kept walking until she blended into the shadows. Patrick picked up his pace to catch up with her again. *How does she move so fast?*

The click of heels against the hardwood floor gave him the only indication she was there. He glanced to either side and saw nothing but book-filled shelves rising in cliff-like peaks, overbearing, oppressive. "I'm lost in a maze, to be certain."

"Over here."

Turning his focus to the sound of her voice, he looked deep into the obscure darkness. There was nothing but gloom and a slight movement contained within the shadows. His skin crawled, and Patrick rubbed his arms absently as if doing so would bring enough circulation to warm the chill that crept over his body. Suddenly, the clicking footsteps stopped. Patrick froze in place, afraid to move in the heavy blackness that plagued the space where he stood.

"Where? Are you there?"

His voice sounded weak, tremulous.

"Yes," she breathed. Patrick was unable to make out just where she stood. It sounded as if her voice floated from everywhere. "This is the door."

"Where are we? What door?"

"The archives," she whispered.

A chill ran down his back again, when suddenly, something snapped and the room was instantly bathed in light. Patrick blinked a few times to adjust to its brilliance. He lifted a hand to his brow as if doing so would lessen the intensity. A single bulb hung from the center of a low ceiling. *Too bright for such a tiny room*, he thought. Patrick blinked again and saw the woman standing to one side, hands clasped in front of her as her eyes stared, unblinking, at him. She did not seem at all bothered by the light.

"My name is Eliza Mary Muir, but you may call me Melissa," she said, and smiled again.

"Melissa. Okay." He glanced around the room as his eyes adjusted further to the light. Buried in stacks of glass cases were documents and books with covers that looked like they would crumble at the slightest touch. An aroma of decay lingered. "Where did that come from? Melissa, I mean? Why not Mary? That's a sweet name. The mother of Jesus was named Mary—doesn't get better than that," he joked, hoping to lighten the mood.

Melissa sighed. Apparently, she didn't find his jokes funny. No doubt, she'd explained her name before. "Eliza Mary is a very old name. There's some history attached to it, with my ancestry. I wanted something bright and a bit more contemporary, I suppose, so I picked Melissa when I was still a little girl." She pointed to an arched doorway on the other side of the room. "Here we are."

Patrick stared at it and a dark, foreboding feeling washed over him. The door was dark, nearly as black as the feeling he had staring at it. Something sinister was hidden behind the door, and Patrick questioned whether he should be the one to unearth it.

"Are you all right, Patrick? You look rather pale, all of the sudden."

He cleared his throat and forced himself to look at one of the glass cases on the other side of the room. "Yes. A little tired, perhaps. It's been quite a long week."

The nervous chuckle escaping his throat did little to convince Melissa he was telling the truth.

"Hmmm." She stared at him for a moment, then turned her back, unlocked the door, and pushed against the mahogany. Tarnished brass hinges groaned, begging not to be disturbed. Patrick guessed the door had not been opened for a very long time.

He inspected the curve of the doorway before moving. A solid oak door, weathered to a deep coffee color, yawned at an angle. It proved a formidable barrier between himself and whatever lay behind it. Inside, the entire room had been built from large stones that had obviously been set in place centuries ago. Rows of the glass cases rested stacked on top of each other, and piled against the stones—a crypt filled with antiquities.

"What's in there?" Patrick could not look away.

TWELVE

H. Hall was etched in the stone, obviously carved with an instrument that was rather rudimentary and probably only found in museums. Most likely, it was a tool used to create the names on grave markers.

There was no question—the lettering looked the same as he'd seen on most tombstones, and Patrick felt as if he were about to enter a tomb. In a way, it was a crypt—one that held the remains of ancient records. The history of the Sullivan House entombed.

"After you," Patrick said. A wave of regret washed over him as soon as the words left his mouth. In truth, he didn't want to go into the vault, but he couldn't back out now.

Melissa stepped inside. "Please follow me, and watch your step."

Patrick hesitated, but in that moment, a light clicked on to illuminate the interior of a vault. He descended two steps made from the same stone as the walls and caught his breath as the heady scent of decay hit him. Sweet almond and festering plant-life mixed with a moldy odor—the smell of decomposing flowers in a funeral home.

"Welcome to the archives." Melissa gestured to the shelves and smiled sweetly. Her face seemed less pale within the vault.

This isn't right. Patrick knew he should listen to his gut, but his rational voice brushed it off as having the jitters. He couldn't let Melissa see that he was scared—particularly as she obviously wasn't.

An air of innocence hovered about her, and Patrick found himself feeling somewhat guilty for not being more of a gentleman. She had been nothing but courteous with him—perhaps too courteous—the kind of courtesy morticians dole out when they express empathy. Fake sentiment—just like his attorney. Everything was a sham meant to keep him distracted from the truth. This time, Patrick refused to be played the fool. He'd find out what the secret of the Sullivan House was even if it was the last thing he ever did. *Two can play this game.*

He forced a toothy grin and sugarcoated his tone. "Thanks."

"Yes, well, we'll need to keep the door shut—after you have settled into your research, of course. The humidity destroys the paper, as you must know. Let me help you find what you need first and then I'll step out to give you privacy for your work."

"Oh, that's not necessary," Patrick remarked a little too loudly. "I mean… I don't require privacy, just the history of the… house, you know."

"Yes, indeed." Melissa turned to a shelf covered in cobwebs. "Not many come down here."

"I wouldn't think so. It's rather gloomy, kinda creepy."

She brushed away the webs with her hand, and Patrick thought he heard her whisper something. Plucking a large leather volume from the shelf, she blew the dust from its cover and carried it over to a small desk. "Creepy to those who've never been in a vault before." She handed Patrick a pair of white gloves. "Please use these when touching the pages."

"Of course." Patrick quickly pulled a glove over each hand. "Could you sit with me, maybe? To help me with this?"

Melissa cocked her head to one side and studied Patrick for a moment. She then turned on her heel and walked toward the door. "Of course. But I must set up the room to accommodate our presence first." She stepped outside.

Within moments, a large fan kicked on some-where inside the ceiling, blowing dust motes and stale air into the vault. Patrick glanced up at the ventilation duct overhead and wondered if he was about to be gassed with something toxic. The smell suggested he might be. He looked to the door and thought about making a mad dash for the exit, but as he stood, Melissa appeared once again through the doorway. She calmly closed the door behind her, sealing them both in the library's tomb that housed artifacts.

"There," she said, and crossed to where he stood at the desk. The book lay untouched on its surface. She glanced at the book, then at Patrick. "Did you have a question?"

"No... I..." He searched for a reasonable explanation as to why he hadn't yet opened the large leather-bound volume. "I'm not sure where to look, actually."

"Let's begin with the Sullivan House." Melissa gracefully slipped on a pair of white gloves, as well. Lowering herself into one of the chairs positioned against the desk, she opened the book's cover and turned the first page. Her voice dropped to almost a whisper. "Why are you interested in that house?"

It was a good question, and Patrick wasn't completely certain he had a descent answer. He dropped his gaze to the opened page and scanned the Table of Contents listed there. Underneath one heading, he saw the words that pricked his interest: *Hidden Treasure*.

"I guess I'm interested in the rumors of treasure."

"Ah... the secret of the Sullivan House. Intriguing, isn't it?" She turned the page. "That is the very reason so many have sought residency within its walls but none have ever found it... or so they say."

"Who says?"

"Well, those who have emerged." Melissa looked up at Patrick. Her gaze was soft, though her eyes were pale and cool. Mesmerized, Patrick could not look away from her. He felt himself being drawn into her, into the peace that surrounded her very being. He wanted to touch her, blend his spirit with hers—he wanted to kiss her.

"I… I'm sorry, what did you say?" Patrick tore his eyes from hers and forced himself to look the yellowed page. "Emerge?"

"Few there be who return from the Sullivan House." Melissa's voice had taken on a somber pitch. It was as if voicing the implied would wake the stories buried within the walls of the vault. She glanced around the room as if to confirm it.

"Why?"

"It's uncertain whether the supposed treasure is physical or maybe something else. No one knows, really."

"Well, I'm going to find out, then I'll come back and tell you all about it."

Melissa said nothing and returned to the book. With one finger, she tapped the top of a page. Scrolled in loopy handwriting were words he had seen before.

The Sullivan House.

The ink, a coppery color placed there by a quill and a steady hand, had bled along the edges of some of the letters. Patrick's breath caught. The handwriting was the same as the invitation that had arrived in his name.

"When was this written… this book?" He stood abruptly, knocking over the chair he'd been sitting in, and pointed at the book as he backed away from it.

"Is there something wrong?"

"That writing… I received an invitation in the same handwriting earlier today."

Melissa smiled. "Many have copied this script for use with the Sullivan House correspondence. That is the magic of digital software, as you know."

Patrick swallowed. *Of course… it's a duplicate of the font. Idiot!* He moved back to the desk, righted his chair, and took a seat. "I'm sorry. It's just that…"

"You seem rather distressed. Perhaps another day would be better?"

"No, please. I'm tired, is all. Please show me what's written here." He motioned for her to continue.

Melissa nodded and began to recite the information recorded on the page.

"As you can see, this was written centuries ago. It's somewhat difficult to read, but those of us who have lived here for years have studied the history of Savannah and know what her residents have said about the city, the people, and of course, the Sullivan House. It's as if we are a part of history. Long ago…" She trailed off, lost somewhere that Patrick could not go. He waited for her to return. After a moment, she glanced at him and smiled.

"I'm sorry. Let me continue. The Sullivan House was built in the early 1600s, but no one is certain by whom—it just suddenly seemed to exist. The land was inhabited by immigrants who settled here, mainly Londoners, lowland Scots, and some Irish—most of whom were convicts. They had been set free in the bog running along the western-most coastal areas.

"One of these was a convicted murderer by the name of Cailech Suileabhain. He had been taken from his family as a young lad and traded to the English as human cargo for slave labor. Upon the ship's arrival, he was to be one of the Irish boys sold to the highest bidder. Those who could tame the coastline in what would be soon known as New America would become these poor boys' masters.

"When the ship landed in the New World, the captives disembarked, chained together. Cailech was never found on board, and as the human cargo was branded and documented, the number fell short.

"Somehow, the boy had disappeared." She paused and looked up at Patrick, studying him before dropping her attention back to the book.

"What happened to him?"

Melissa shrugged. "Slowly, over the next six months, the bodies of the slave owners were found strung up by their hands, their corpses burned beyond recognition. No one knew who had done such horrific acts upon the British settlers. But, interestingly, it all began soon after Cailech's ship had arrived. Not long afterward, an Irish taskmaster was found in the same state—brutally tortured to death."

Patrick shifted in his seat and cleared his throat. "I don't see how this has anything to do with the Sullivan House. I'm really more interested in the house as…"

Melissa held a finger in the air to silence him. "I'm getting to that. Please bear with me." She paused for a moment, smiling pretentiously. "Word soon spread that the mysteriously missing Cailech had cursed the slave owners along these shores: 'He who tortures the innocent shall surely suffer the same, times ten.' Fear spread amongst the people, and the Irish slaves were treated worse for it.

"Then, one night, a young boy who claimed to be Cailech's friend was found—his body hung from a tree. The body's head had been severed at the neck and propped upon a tree branch as a warning… or so they thought.

"The next day, the decapitated slave's master, his wife, and three of his household, were found with their heads on a spike, lining their massive estate's iron gates."

Patrick stood. "While your story is very entertaining, I still don't see how it has anything to do with why I'm here."

Melissa smiled again, slowly this time. "It was said that Cailech Suileabhain roams the night to extract revenge. The Sullivan House has been a house of recompense ever since."

Melissa sat with her hands folded in her lap. She stared at Patrick and her gaze chilled him worse that the story she had told.

"And the Sullivan House is this estate you speak of? Named after the missing boy?" Patrick sat back down.

"That's what some believe."

"So, there's a ghost at the Sullivan House?"

Melissa chuckled. "There's a curse. The house is… well, again, a place for restitution, per se. They say that those who are most troubled in life go there for respite."

Patrick turned the page, but his eyes didn't focus on the image sketched there. "I don't believe in curses or ghosts… or treasure, for that matter."

Melissa nodded. "Then why are you so insistent on finding it?"

"Perhaps it's just something to do—something out of the ordinary. An adventure, so to speak, and I need a good adventure."

"Good for you, then." She sighed. "Not many years later, a monk was found inside the house. He had been crucified…"

"*What?*" Patrick's head shot up. He locked eyes with Melissa.

"…nailed in a perfect crucifixion against the ceiling. No one knew how long his body had been up there. Interestingly, it was discovered that this same monk had falsely accused a young girl of witchcraft and nailed her to a cross to purge her soul of evil just before he burned her alive."

Patrick grimaced and looked down at the book.

"Written in blood next to his body were the words: *Tá Cúiteamh Mianach. C. S.*" The smile never left her face.

"What does that mean?" Patrick swallowed against the bile that rose in the back of his throat.

"Vengeance is mine." Melissa smiled. "Essentially, recompense shall be given." She pointed to the inscription. "The signature is: *C. S.*"

"Coincidence… pure coincidence. I'm surprised no one's exposed this yet. C. S. could be anyone. The fact that the murdered monk was found inside the Sullivan House was merely coincidental."

"Think about it. C. S. Cailesh Sullivan."

"You're getting your own story mixed up, Melissa. You said his name was Suileabhain. I thought you said it was Suileabhain. Here, it's written here." Patrick pointed to the same signature at the bottom of the page.

"Suileabhain is the old Gaelic name for Sullivan. It's assumed the 'C.' stands for Cailech, although, you are correct. No one knows for certain," she said then added, "You know, Sullivan means 'eye,' as in 'All Seeing Eye.' It's said that there are no secrets kept within the Sullivan House."

"Then what is this?" Patrick said and waved a hand over the open book. "What is the 'Secret of the Sullivan House?' What the hell is this bloody book talking about?"

Melissa smiled. "Apparently, there is something secret buried within the house itself. No one knows for sure. Those who enter rarely leave. Perhaps the secret is the serenity there—its residents choose to say until death takes them from the house."

Patrick looked at Melissa. "That's absurd. There has to be something else… maybe an actual treasure buried by that dead monk. I mean, why would anyone want to stay in a place with a history like that?" He tapped the open book. "Not unless there really is a treasure buried there? Maybe this Cailech stashed gold and silver he looted from the people he murdered. Maybe he was just a greedy murderer collecting a hefty retirement for himself."

"Perhaps." Melissa's voice suddenly warmed though her smile dropped. "In good conscience, I must offer my advice, Patrick."

"Buy a sharp pick and shovel?" He attempted a weak chuckle, but his voice failed. Melissa didn't laugh.

"Don't go there. Stay away from that place. It's not worth what you seek."

"You don't know what I seek. I told you, I don't believe in ghosts and I'm not easily scared away, once my mind is set." He looked at her and sighed. "Look, I'm just an average guy looking for a really good investment in real estate. Maybe even the possibility of starting over again. I appreciate your advice, Melissa, really, I do. But you have no idea what my intentions are."

"I know that others have sought the same. Things did not fare well for them." She stared off into the distance. "Perhaps it's what's meant to be. Perhaps recompense awaits us all in some form or other." There was a moment of silence before she snapped to. "Something awaits you inside the Sullivan House, else you wouldn't have received the invitation. Again, my advice: don't go."

"So there is treasure!" He fisted the air and began to pace.

Melissa stood, gently closing the book, then removing her gloves. "Yes, there *is* something inside the house. But…" She looked at him with pleading eyes.

"The treasure! The gold this Sullivan kid stole over years and years. No one's found it because they don't know *how* to find it." He grinned and plucked the gloves from his own hands, placed his palms on each of her cheeks, and kissed her on each cheek. "I'll find it, though. It's a gift… 'serendipity,' as my attorney calls it. Thank you!"

"Patrick." Melissa took hold of his sleeve. "Don't…"

Something about her eyes or voice—he couldn't be sure—made him want to kiss her again. But the coolness of her skin, her mien, gave him the impression the vault contained something detestable—an impression secreted away within the archaic history contained inside a library crypt.

THIRTEEN

"I S HE SLEEPING?" THE VOICE was but a whisper—a breath in the wind that blew from distant trees and the deep night outside the window.

"Yes."

"Why isn't he with us, Mommy?"

"It was his choice to send us alone," she replied, and turned to face the window.

"How do you know he's sleeping?"

She turned, smiled at her little one, and sighed. "Because his chest rises. See there?" She pointed to the bed but quickly turned her face back to the window. "We should leave him now."

"But I don't want to go. I want to stay and watch him."

The little girl bent down, closing the narrow gap between herself and the bed. She stared at his face and watched with fascination as he took deep breaths, then exhaled with a snort. Reaching a tiny hand to his cheek, she held it there and felt the warmth of his skin. The mother stepped into a corner and veiled herself in the shadows that lingered there.

"Come, child. We must go."

"But why don't we sleep?"

"Because," the mother whispered and held her hand out to the little girl. The girl turned from the bed and followed her mother into the shadows.

"But why?"

"Because your chest doesn't rise any longer."

FOURTEEN

Patrick awoke with a start. He glanced at the corner of his hotel room, but there was only darkness. *A dream?* He raised a hand to his face—one side felt ice cold. *She touched me.* He glanced at the clock that read 6:06:06.

"Six-six-six again. What the hell?" He shifted his gaze to the window. Rotted drapes blew freely in a soft wind that whispered words he could not understand. A chill ran along his spine.

"Definitely a bad dream," Patrick said and rolled over, tucking the bed sheet over his head to block out anything that stood in the room with him. He could still feel eyes staring at him from the shadowed corner. "Who's there?" he said from beneath the sheet, but there was no answer, only the wind. Lifting the linen from his face, he looked back at the dark corner.

Nothing.

"This is bullshit!" he said aloud. "Leave me alone."

The clock clicked, indicating the minutes had changed. Patrick looked at it—6:06:06. Nothing had changed. Suddenly, the radio snapped on and static broke the silence of the still dark room.

Daddy…

He'd heard it—a faint whisper within the white noise playing over the radio. Patrick slapped the radio off, jumped from his bed, and darted into the bathroom. There was no way he'd shower… not in this room. He quickly brushed his teeth, keeping his eyes averted from the mirror or anything else that might reflect images he did not want to see. The wind howled against the bathroom window and he clapped his hands over his ears, shutting out all sound. The wind still found him. Grabbing hold of his belongings, he shoved everything into his bag and slammed it shut.

Daddy.

The radio had flipped on again and the white noise grew louder. Patrick tossed a few bills onto the dresser and walked out. Room 6 closed its door behind him and the static fell silent.

FIFTEEN

THE AIR WAS MUGGY EVEN without the sun to warm it, and though the wind blew, the thermometer showed 83 F recorded on its stem. Still, Patrick shivered as he stood there in the dank morning. Gathering his senses, he tried to figure out what to do next. There would be no sleep for the rest of the morning, so the next best thing would be coffee.

He walked to his car and hopped in. As he turned on the car, the radio came on—static again. Patrick quickly shut it off and glanced up at the room he'd been in. Blue light sputtered inside, illuminating the window with an eerie afterglow. Perhaps he'd left the television on. *Static makes that color, and Lord knows, that's all that happens in that stinkin' room.* He blinked and thought he saw movement. *No!*

A tiny face stared back at him—wispy and transparent. Beside her stood a woman—the face was all too familiar.

"Heather? What the hell do you want?" Patrick shouted and slammed the hatchback into reverse.

Gravel and dust was kicked up in front of the head-lights as he pulled away, distancing himself from Room Six. Daring one last look, his eyes darted to the window just briefly to watch as both faces slowly receded into the darkness. Patrick shifted again and tore off toward the only place he'd felt safe since his arrival yesterday.

Fortunately, the lights blazed brightly inside the diner as he pulled up. "No static here," he said as he parked his car.

As if it were the only refuge left on the outskirts of Savannah, Patrick leapt from his car and ran to the door. It was locked, but he could see movement inside behind the counter. He pounded his fist on the glass. The waitress from the night before walked up and shook her head.

"I've got to come in!" he shouted through the glass.

She pointed to the sign that read Hours: *7 AM to 11 PM* and shook her head again. Patrick pulled a twenty-dollar bill from his pocket and pressed it against the glass. Within moments, the door was unlocked and Patrick was seated with a cup of coffee. The waitress walked over and set a steaming scone down in front of him.

"What is going on with you?" she finally asked. She delivered a small cup of cream and some sugar to the table. "What couldn't wait another ten minutes until we open, anyway? I don't get paid for this, you know."

"That's why the crisp twenty before I walked in." Patrick gave her a *don't press my buttons* look.

She glanced at the bill tucked inside her apron pocket, sighed, and sat down across from him in the booth. "My name is Shari." She poured herself a cup and lowered her gaze to stare at him under heavy eyelids. "You look like you've seen a ghost, yeah?"

"Patrick."

Shari cleared her throat and spoke in hushed tones. "Look, I don't know what kind of trouble you're in, but this isn't the place to bring it. Screven's Point is… different, if you know what I mean." She glanced around as if someone could hear her.

"Is that what this town is called? Screven's Point?"

She nodded and then shifted her eyes to the library. "Suburb of Savannah, kinda. Did you go in there, last night?"

Patrick followed her lead and looked through the window to the elaborate, decayed building. It was dark and silent. *A little action from that place left my heart pounding for a good reason.* He nodded. "Yeah."

"Did you find what you were looking for?" Shari asked and leaned in. Clearly, this waitress was used to gathering juicy gossip, and Patrick was her latest quest for something delicious. "You can trust me."

"I don't even know you."

"My name is Ruth… Ruth Mae Sorrel, but everybody calls me Shari. Ruth sounds too old, and my granddaughter can't say her *R*s very well, so she started calling me 'Gamma Shari.' Not sure why. My granddad several generations back fought in the Civil War."

Patrick looked at her. *What a strange bird.* He pushed the thought away and forced a smile. "Good for him. I'm thinking of settling down here."

"Why?" Shari drew back. "There's nothing for a guy like you here in Screven's Point. There's nothing for anyone here." Her face blanched.

"Why not?" Patrick eyed her and sensed there was something she knew—something she would never tell, no matter how much she loved to spread gossip. Shari wore the same expression the two salty dogs had worn in the pub when he'd mentioned the Sullivan House. Something important about that house was being kept under wraps, and Patrick was going to find out what it was. "What's wrong with settling down in Screven's Point? You're here, aren't you?"

"Because a nice young man like you needs to get out and make something of himself… not here… not in Screven's Point. This is a dead end, Patrick."

"I just left a dead end, Shari. I need a new place—a new beginning—and I think I've found some real estate that might suit me just fine."

The sun crested the top of the library and, along with it, Patrick's self-confidence. The night had brought nothing but paranoia, likely caused by too much caffeine, greasy food, and bad coffee with an attorney at the courthouse. This was a new day, and Patrick was determined to make the best of it.

"Don't, Patrick." Shari placed a clammy hand over his.

"Why?"

"Because this is a sick town, and that house is the cancer that's caused it."

"You're rather dramatic, aren't you, Shari?" Patrick grinned.

"You don't understand. There's history in that place. People go in and never come out. Some say the devil himself lives there. I've heard some tell they see that monk walking around at night inside. They see him from the windows. Blood drips from the ceiling sometimes."

"Oh, come on!"

"Okay, we'll, maybe not the blood part, but the monk is real. Found him nailed to the ceiling. God knows how long he'd been up there. The old man found him, and they say it messed him up good."

Patrick leaned in. "What old man?"

"The one that owns the antique store down the road. Wilson is his name, I think."

"Wilkins."

"You've met him?"

"Yeah." Patrick glanced back at the library. He made a mental note to visit Wilkins.

"Look, you're a nice guy, and there aren't many of those left anymore. Stay away from that house. Go home to your family. Live your life and forget this place." She took a sip from her cup. "I gotta get back to work." Standing up, she adjusted her apron and paused to take one last look at Patrick. "Take my advice, Patrick, please."

"I'll be fine, Shari. I'm going to start over here. It'll be great. And, besides, I'm your new best customer." He set another twenty on the table and got up. "See you tonight for supper. I'll have the meatloaf with a baked potato and green beans. That looks fabulous." He pointed to a poster on the wall displaying a glossy photo of an oversized plate with meat and a potato. Someone had drawn steam rising from them.

Shari watched him walk toward the door, her face drawn, the lines between her eyebrows furrowed. "Please don't."

"It's all good, Shari." Patrick refused to notice anything but the sunshine outside and tapped his forehead in salute. "Oh, and don't forget the barbeque sauce," he added, walking out of the diner.

Shari watched him get into his car and make the turn down Bull Street, her face still white and hands still clammy as they clutched the twenty. As he disappeared, she swallowed, then whispered under her breath:

"You don't know what you've done."

SIXTEEN

NO ONE ANSWERED HIS CALL, and since the door was unlocked, Patrick thought nothing of walking inside. It was a business, after all. Shouldn't businesses encourage their customers to enter? That was the rationale Patrick used as he strolled through the antiquities store.

"Wilkins? Anyone here?"

His voice echoed against the walls decorated with stuffed heads and blank eyes that stared at him as he passed by. Patrick ran his fingertips over a glass case as he stared at a baboon's head mounted on a cracked plaque. Its teeth were menacingly sharp, and its coal-black eyes seemed to glint with life—an improbability for taxidermy.

"Norman Bates would feel right at home in this place," Patrick said under his breath. "Wilkins!" he shouted, but there was no response. As he neared the back of the store, the light faded and, though Patrick sought a switch, there was nothing available to light the room. He stepped into the darkness.

Shadows speckled the room, bringing odd dimensions to the objects that lined the walls and lay scattered along the floor. His pace slowed. Patrick saw a face and jumped backward, stumbling over rolled-up carpet. As he turned toward it, he recognized his own distorted image framed in the glass of a beveled mirror.

"Shit!"

He stepped over the carpet roll and moved toward ancient furniture grouped together. Next to the mirror, a scattered row of photos was lined up above the antique dressers and settees. It was made to look like a sitting room, he figured, but instead, the grouping looked more like a funeral parlor. He took another step and caught sight of a side table with a top tier that was stained from use as a pipe-holder.

Speckling the small shelf, several medals with faded silk ribbons were on display. Each one bore the shape of the Celtic cross and was made out of gold. Set in the center was an etched soldier's helmet with plums carved intricately within the precious metal. Three letters lined the far edges of a shield below: F C B.

Patrick lifted one of the medals and turned it over. Scrolled on the back in hand-lettered script was a name and date:

Knights of Adrestia
1818

Patrick measured the weight in his palm, and a smile crossed his lips. Glancing around, he encountered only the empty stares of the dead animals hanging on the walls.

"You won't be needing this, and I'm guessing the old man won't miss it," he said and dropped the medal into a pocket. As he was about to lift another, a shadow passed across the glass covering one of the photos. Patrick jumped. "Who's there?"

The room remained silent, dark, and restless. He stared at the photo, and it seemed alive, as well. Leaning in to get a better look, Patrick saw a face staring back at him. He jumped, turned around, and stared at an empty room.

"Get it together, Pat," he said and turned back to the photo. The image was old, cracked, but perfectly preserved otherwise. Three children sat on stools next to a woman. All of them were dressed in black and appeared to be sleeping. Only one child kept her terrified eyes open. Below the photo, the words *Memento Mori* were written in ink with the same loopy letters. "The invitation…" Patrick breathed. His name had been written with the same script. He set the photo down.

"Remember the dead." Patrick stumbled and fell backward. Icy hands caught him and he gasped, nearly fainting from the sound of an unwelcomed voice.

"*Remember you must also die* is the literal translation." Wilkins pressed his skeletal fingers into Patrick's arm as he helped him back to his feet.

"What the hell? Why would you do that?" Patrick's constricted throat would not allow his voice to rise above a breathy rasp, though he felt as if he were shouting.

"I thought you would want to know what it means." Wilkins released Patrick's arm, stepped back, and clasped both hands in front of him.

"No, I mean, why did you sneak up on me like that?"

Wilkins smiled with thin lips and waited patiently while Patrick lowered himself onto one of the settees. "Perhaps you were too engrossed in pecuniary things."

"I… I didn't hear you approach. I was looking around at…"

"Yes, I saw your interest in our photo collection." Wilkins' focus moved up to the wall and his face relaxed almost lovingly as his gaze moved from photo to photo. "These are photographs of the dead. Oh, some of the subjects are living, but most are deceased. Aren't they a beautiful representation?"

"No! Not lovely at all. You keep pictures of dead people in here?" Patrick wrung his hands. "Well, you keep dead animals, so why shouldn't I be surprised? Maybe there's a corpse hidden away in one of these cases too." He stood and began to pace, his look darting from Wilkins to the wall display.

"This is a business of antiquities, as I explained before. Everything in here has passed on—the decorum, lifestyle, jewelry…" Wilkins paused. "Even badges of award." His eyes dropped to Patrick's pocket.

Patrick turned his back. "Yeah, well, everything is old and dead in here." He pointed to the photos. "Dead people's faces are plastered on your wall? What kind of sick bastard are you?"

Wilkins sighed and took Patrick by the arm, gently escorting him toward the front of the store. Patrick shook off Wilkins grip but followed him anyway. "We all die, Patrick. It's part of our existence. Things die too. But death brings beauty with it—particularly to objects that age. Those photos, for example—most families couldn't afford photography services during the 19th century. In a desperate move to preserve memories, those poor families would pay dearly for a photograph. Anything to hold onto a memorial of their loved one—even in death. As you can see, they went to great lengths to re-create the image of a happy, living family."

"They're dead! It's the most macabre thing I've ever seen!"

"The photos are priceless. You don't see these nowadays. Mostly, its value came as it was the only memento of a beloved family member—especially since the dead one was placed in the ground soon afterward." Wilkins' voice sounded icy. "Don't you treasure the photos you have with your loved ones? The photos of your family will only become more valuable to you over the coming years, don't you agree?"

"My family is dead!"

"Exactly my point." Wilkins grinned.

"I don't want any pictures of a dead wife and daughter. Are you insane?" Patrick stopped pacing and faced the old man. He wasn't sure if his agitation was due to anger or the chill in Wilkins' voice.

"Macabre, perhaps. Insane? That's a matter of perspective." Wilkins paused to straighten one of the photos. "With regards to your family, why not capture a permanent memory of their last moments on this earth?"

"Because they were murdered. Cold-blooded murder. Why would I want to capture a memory of their dead, mutilated bodies? I'm trying to forget." Patrick strode to the door.

"Yes, I suppose you are. Tell me…" Wilkins followed him as far as the counter. "…why did you come here, Patrick?"

Patrick paused with his hand on the knob and took a deep breath. Turning on his heels, he paused to face Wilkins and glared at him through slits. "I came here to negotiate a deal with you, old man."

Wilkins smiled and trailed the fingers of one hand across the glass case. "Ah, I see. And what negotiations are those?" He swallowed. The bump in his bony throat rose, then fell. Patrick relaxed a bit and smiled at Wilkins.

"I want to buy the Sullivan House."

SEVENTEEN

A SQUAD CAR WAS PARKED in the circular drive. Its lights were off, though the engine was running. Painted along the side was the occupant's title: *Medical Examiner*. Patrick stared at the bowed head sitting in the driver's seat and wondered why an M.E. would be parked outside the Sullivan House.

He opened the door of his own vehicle and stepped onto the gravel that lined the drive leading up to the mansion. The last thing Patrick wanted was trouble. Associated with the Sullivan House were too many stories—too much history. This was not a story he wanted added to his newest investment. Patrick took a deep breath and watched from where he stood.

Standing to one side of the M.E.'s car was a lanky man wearing a fedora, and next to him, stood Wilkins. He glanced up at Patrick but did not otherwise acknowledge his arrival. Patrick looked around for the familiar red truck, but it was nowhere to be seen. *Wilkins needs to know who is boss now. I guess today's that day.* He took a deep breath and strode toward the M.E.'s vehicle.

"What's going on here?" Patrick said as he approached them.

Wilkins peered at him and forced a thin-lipped grin that looked more like a grimace. "James, let me introduce you to the new owner of the Sullivan House," he said to the man standing next to him. "Patrick, this is James Devonshire—the town's medical examiner. James, please meet Patrick."

Patrick shook the man's hand and glanced to the figure sitting in the front seat. He was writing something on a clipboard.

"My assistant, Jacob," Devonshire said, following Patrick's stare. "He digs the graves."

"Call me Jake." The voice sounded muffled from the front seat, although he never looked up from his writing.

"Why are you here?" Patrick directed his comment to Devonshire.

"Death inside." Devonshire glanced at the house.

"What happened?"

"Oh, nothing really. This is just protocol." He motioned to Jake. "A young lady died in there some-time last night. My job is to pronounce her dead and try to determine cause—although it's obvious. She's been dead for a while." He chuckled and glanced at Wilkins, who responded with the same grimace.

"For a while? Nobody noticed?" Patrick shot Wilkins a look.

"When they go that young, we have to do an autopsy anyway. It's protocol. But everyone knows how she went. Drugs kill—well, you know the saying."

"What young lady?" Patrick took a step forward.

Wilkins nodded, keeping his eyes on the house. "It's most unfortunate."

"What young lady!"

"One of the residents, Patrick. Remember that I mentioned on occasion there are residents who…?" Wilkins began, but Patrick cut him off.

"I remember what you said, Wilkins. Where is she? Did they get the body out?" Patrick was beginning to feel uneasy. "We're supposed to be doing an inspection of the property, and I walk into this? A dead girl, and the Medical Examiner talking like it's an everyday occurrence! What is going on around here?"

"Relax, please, Mr. Donovan." Patrick glared at Wilkins. His use of a formal title didn't sit well. "This is just protocol for an unfortunate event. We will still conduct our inspection today," Wilkins added.

"I didn't plan on a dead girl interfering with our plans."

"We'll be done here in a few. She'll be buried before nightfall." Devonshire nodded to a plot of lawn next to the house.

"I thought you were going to do an autopsy?" Patrick's fists balled up at his sides. "Blowin' off protocol, are we, Devonshire?"

"Not at all. We'll submit our paperwork—Wilkins signed for it since there's no next of kin and everyone knows she was a user—and if we need to, we'll dig her back up and do it then."

"*What?*" Patrick shot a look at Wilkins, who glanced to the cemetery and sighed.

"Doing it this way saves money on funeral expenses for a woman who has no one to pay, and no family to claim the body. It also saves the state money on an unnecessary autopsy when the cause of death is obvious."

"I don't like this, Wilkins. Not one bit! I don't want a bunch of fresh bodies buried in my backyard, either!" Patrick looked at the graveyard and the freshly dug hole there.

The entire area was enclosed by a low-set iron fence that had spikes every foot or so as if placed in warning. It was easy to see that no one would be kept out by its barbs—stepping over the two-foot railing would be an easy task. Still, there was little doubt that no one in their right mind would do so—crossing the barrier into an estate inhabited by the dead didn't seem wise.

"Now, Mr. Donovan. Where else can she go?" Wilkins acknowledged the gravedigger.

Sagging tombstones and blackened granite archangels dotted the lawn. To one side, heaped in a mound, fresh dirt lined a large hole. Sandy-haired and grimy, the old man inside the hollow lifted another shovel full and dumped it onto the mound.

"He's digging her grave," Patrick stated the obvious.

"Indeed. We bury our dead quickly here—especially those who once inhabited the Sullivan House."

Wilkins glanced up at the sinister mansion's windows. "It's a courtesy bestowed to the residents."

"What?" Patrick was incredulous. "You just throw the bodies into a grave and don't bother with… with…" Patrick stopped and stared at Devonshire. "Where are all these people's families? What's he here for then, if he's not going to do an autopsy?"

"Someone has to pronounce." Devonshire took the clipboard from Jake, examining it momentarily before signing it. "Wilkins can't do it and no one will go in there."

"You're not going to examine the body?"

"Like I said before, we don't need to. She's dead. It's obvious. And there are track marks all up and down her arms and legs. Opening her up won't show anything we don't already know. If the state orders it, we'll dig her up. But they won't." Devonport handed the clipboard back to Jake, then turned to face Wilkins. "Well, I'm finished here. We'll leave the rest to Benjamin there." He looked at the gravedigger, who lifted another shovel of dirt out of the hole.

"This is insane!" Patrick's eyes went from the house to Jake's clipboard to Benjamin. "Freakin' insane!"

Moments later, the medical examiner's car turned off the gravel road and made its way through the deep canopy of trees that led to town. Patrick stared, lost in thought, at the dust cloud kicked up by the car until his attention snapped around to the commotion coming from the front of the house.

Benjamin had finished his digging and was holding one end of a sheet. The other end was supported by a scrawny fellow who stared wide-eyed at their cargo as he followed Benjamin's lead. Taking slow, measured steps, they made their way down the front porch staircase. With each step, the bundle shifted, requiring the men to adjust its weight as they hauled it to the newly dug grave.

"Hey," Patrick called out, jogging over to them. "Wait! I need to talk to you." As he approached the entry, he stopped, surveying the best way to enter. The iron gate that marked the neglected entrance to the cemetery was overgrown with vines. Someone had forced it open recently, ripping the vines from their roots. Following fresh footprints, Patrick stepped through and marched up to the open grave. "You can't just put a body in there."

Benjamin glanced around the plot and then looked at Wilkins. His scrawny helper stared without blinking at Patrick. "Where do you want us to put it, then?"

"I mean… how do I know…?" Patrick fumbled with the question.

Without uttering a word, Benjamin pulled back the sheet to reveal a purple face, its eyes wide open and bleary, a slack jaw, and opened mouth. "She's dead, all right. That lady from inside."

Patrick gasped and nearly stumbled over a grave marker that had sunk down deep in the earth behind him.

"Died sometime last week, they think, although nobody knew it 'cuz she was all alone in there, you know," Benjamin stated rather matter-of-factly.

"No one found her? She died alone?"

"Yup, but Jeb, here, found her when the dog wouldn't stop barkin' this mornin'. He followed it to the door and knocked, but there was no answer. Except he could hear someone cryin' inside and heard voices saying, 'Help.'" Benjamin looked at the lanky fellow, who nodded, his focus glued to the body.

"Said, 'Help me' so soft-like I could barely hear it. Then the dog ran off an'…" Jeb started, but Benjamin cut him off.

"But then you called Mr. Wilkins, didn't you, Jeb?" Benjamin said, and leveled a dark look at him.

Jeb nodded. "My job to call Wilkins when somethin' happens. I cain't go in thar 'less he's here too."

"Cover her up," Patrick snapped and walked back toward the place he'd seen Wilkins last. He was nowhere to be seen. "Wilkins! Don't you run off and hide from me. Not now!"

"He drove off with the med'cal examiner and Jake." Benjamin stared at Patrick, the sheet still suspended between himself and Jeb. It swayed in the breeze like a heavy white hammock.

"I don't remember seeing him get in the car with them."

Benjamin just shrugged. "Do you want us to bury this someplace else?"

"No. I mean, where? I can't believe she's not in a coffin or something decent… just a sheet!"

"Too expensive."

Patrick shot Benjamin a look just as he and Jeb dropped the bundle into the grave. The sheet fell away from her head and shoulders, exposing eyes that stared at an earthy wall lining her final resting place. Patrick glanced down at the face again and gagged. Bloated green patches wept liquid from parts of her skin. The rest had an odd red sheen that made the body look almost waxy. Obviously, she'd been dead for a very long time. In spite of the decay setting in, he recognized her as the woman he'd seen sitting on the front porch steps the day before.

Patrick covered his nose with a sleeve. "She just got here… didn't she?"

Benjamin nodded. "Yup. Checked in a few weeks ago, I heard. Most don't make it more than a day or two in there." He tossed the first shovel of dirt into the grave and glanced at the house.

"I… I don't know what that means." Patrick looked toward the Sullivan House. He shifted his weight and tried to appear imposing, despite the alarms in the pit of his stomach. "The house is empty now—my house. You'd best get ready. Things are going to change around here."

"That's what they all say," Jeb piped in. "By the way, that place is never really empty… not ever, not really. Not in the dark… not at night, especially."

Patrick glanced from Jeb to the house and studied the height of the house. He swallowed. There *was* something dark about it—almost as if, with all the death surrounding it, the house was alive… waiting for someone. *Maybe you've made a mistake, Patrick.* He cleared his throat and steadied his nerves. *It's just wood and stone—a treasure that holds something valuable.* Whatever was in there, it belonged to him now.

"The Sullivan House is just valuable real estate. I don't know what you mean, and your efforts to scare me won't work," Patrick said.

"Means people come here to die." Benjamin cut in. He tossed another shovel full and covered the body's face with dirt.

EIGHTEEN

"Just crazy old men," Patrick said under his breath. He glanced at the iron-gated cemetery. Benjamin and Jeb had finished their work and were stomping the last remnants of grass over the newly dug grave. "These guys are called *'fossors'* for a reason—untouchables—gravediggers, for hell's sake! They've got to be a little shy of a full deck to do this job." He shifted the cell phone to his other hand and paused.

He ambled to the front entry and walked the pathway that led to an expansive stairway made of stone. "Hello? Wilkins? Answer your phone!" Patrick pulled the cell phone from his ear and stared at it. "Shit!"

The phone had gone dead. He tucked the phone into a pocket and felt around for the set of keys Wilkins had given him earlier. A sharp prick caught his ring finger. He winced and grasped hold of the offending object, then pulled it out to examine it—along with his bloody fingertip. *KDP* was etched on a Celtic cross. "Oh, yeah, I forgot. Well, here's my badge of ownership,

I suppose." He pinched the bloody fingertip to stop the bleeding. "Knights of Adrestia—you have a new, unofficial member, and he's now the proud resident of the Sullivan House."

A wind gust caught the inside of his jacket, nearly blowing him onto the stones. He put out his hand to catch himself and cursed. Then something else sent a chill down his spine. Eyes were upon him. Someone was watching him from within the house—or perhaps it was the house itself. Patrick paused on the stone stairway and looked skyward at the highest cupola. There, in a darkened window, he saw it—a face.

He pulled his jacket around him as the wind began to beat against the expansive porch. *Get away from here, Patrick.* The voice of reason would not leave his thoughts.

"Hell no! This is mine and I deserve it all!" he said, though the wind swallowed his words. Staring at the window, he looked for the face again, adding, "I don't know who's inside, but there'll be hell to pay once I find you. Damn homesteaders!"

Patrick moved up the staircase and stepped onto the porch. The wind shifted and chilled his bones. Behind him, the soft hiss of air, like a winter wind sucked into an abyss, lifted the hairs of his arms. He turned to see where it was coming from. A shadowy figure stood at the edge of the path, watching him. Patrick opened his mouth, but there was no sound. Just then, lightning cracked and the entire estate was illuminated, casting elongated shadows from the tombstones. Patrick refused to look at them and, instead, kept his eyes glued on the figure. It lifted its arm and shifted its weight. Patrick recognized the face.

"Wilkins!"

Lightning flashed again, this time bringing a torrential downfall with it. *He's come back to send you off. Be polite.* Rain poured over Patrick as he gestured to the old man. As if he hadn't seen him, Wilkins remained unmoved. *You want me to go to you? Why don't you just come up here to get out of the rain, old man?* Patrick waved again. No response. *Fine. Have it your way, Wilkins. I'll come to you, then.*

He'd descend nearly halfway, when suddenly, another blast of lightning cut through the dense canopy and sliced open a towering white pine tree down to the roots. Half of its trunk splintered, casting glowing cinder to the bottom of the stairs where Patrick stood. He leapt out of the way as it landed, showered by cascading burnt bark and embers.

"Good God!" Patrick said and crossed himself absently. The air hissed again and a new sound accompanied it from the house. Creaking against ancient hinges, the front door of the Sullivan House opened. Patrick turned toward it, abandoning Wilkins where he stood in the rain.

In the doorway, the figure of a monk waited, taking up nearly half of the door's entire frame. He wore the robes of a 16th-century Spanish monastery with ebony rosary beads draped across his waist. A gold-and-emerald-encrusted cross hung from his neck. His hands were hidden inside the long sleeves of his robe.

Patrick stared at the monk, glancing from the monk's head to his bare, bloody feet brushed by the shredded hem of his tunic. Gasping, he made the sign of a cross again, mostly out of habit, possibly out of fear. *The crucified monk?* "Who… what are you?"

The monk smiled.

Patrick could scarcely breathe. *Are you alive or dead?* The thought must have made its way to the monk because just then, the cleric nodded.

Patrick looked up again at the monk's face and shuddered. "A ghost…?" The smile dropped from the monk's face and Patrick dropped his focus to the cross hanging about the specter's neck. "What happened to you?" Patrick said, pointing at the monk's feet, though his eyes never left the jeweled relic that hung about the monk's neck. "I… I shouldn't be here. I need to go, really."

The monk lifted the hood from his head and smiled with pale, thin lips buried in fleshy jowls. He motioned for Patrick to follow him inside. Patrick hesitated for a moment, glancing back at Wilkins. He wasn't there. From inside, a compelling pull from the house gripped him. Patrick felt he was attached to a cable that was dragging him into its interior. He wanted to enter, too—that was the mystery of it. Patrick wanted more than anything to be inside the house.

It's that damn cross—reminds you that there's a treasure inside here, Pat. Belongs to you too and this crazy-ass monk obviously knows where it is. Look at the size of those emeralds! The thought snapped Patrick back to reality, and he took a step forward.

The monk nodded in approval, covered his head with the hood, and glided into the interior of the house.

Don't lose this guy, Pat. He's gonna lead you straight to the prize. Patrick's thoughts nearly shouted at him as he took another step. Without thinking, he looked up to the ceiling. Afraid of what he might see, he shielded his eyes with a hand, but still saw the marks there. Stains stood out against the grain, visible in four distinct points—the evidence of something gruesome there a long time ago. *A cross—the crucifixion.*

Tearing his gaze away, he glanced to either side of the foyer's entryway and caught sight of the same stone lions he'd seen at the library. These were set alongside a magnificent staircase that opened into the front entryway. He looked at the lions a bit harder and realized they were made of marble.

That's it. Look at something else. From the corner of his eyes, he saw movement and hoped it was only his escort. *Look away. Look for something else to think about.*

To his right, a single pricket candelabrum stood to one side of the vestibule. Nearly a dozen tapered candles blazed, filling the hall with light that danced from the corners. Ornately carved statues had been placed along the base of a mahogany hall tree. The candle posts were carved images of cherubim with faces that watched him from the doorway. Patrick's eyes darted to the statues—all of them appeared to be made of gold. He took another step.

What are you waiting for? Go in and claim all that is yours.

The voice was not in his head this time—it came like a whisper from somewhere inside the house. Patrick looked down at his feet, ready to take another step, then realized he already stood inside. Just then, the hiss of air closing a final void rushed by as the door to the Sullivan House closed behind him.

NINETEEN

L IGHT BLINKED IN THE WINDOWS covering both sides of an elongated portico as lightning burst across an angry sky. Gargoyles, lining both sides of the ceiling, smiled with pointed teeth. Their faces remained downcast with eyes that watched all who entered the great vestibule of the Sullivan House.

I've been swallowed alive. Patrick shook his head, hoping the thought would disappear, but it didn't.

"Um… where are we going? I'd like to take a moment to inspect the house. Are you with Wilkins?" He fired off questions at the monk, but received no response. The monk continued to walk directly for the staircase, and Patrick dutifully followed behind.

Quickly glancing from side to side, he looked for anything that would appear normal—a telephone or light switch, even. To his right, a doorway had been draped with tapestry that was pulled to one side and tied off with a heavy cord. Facing the center of the room, a fireplace flickered with amber light, indicating a fire had been lit there sometime earlier in the day. Next to it, butting against the wall, stood a highboy in marble and Cherrywood. A service had been set with silver trays filled with fruit, pastries, and various cheeses. To one side, burgundy wine glistened deep maroon through a crystal decanter.

"I need a drink," Patrick said and walked into the room. He lifted the decanter's stopper and poured. Holding the crystal wine goblet under his nose for a moment, he inhaled the sweet scent of very expensive claret. "This smells amazing." Patrick lifted it to his lips, sipping the vintage beverage. "Old too."

"It was brought to the Sullivan House by privateers from Madeira in the late 1700s."

Patrick jumped and dropped his glass. Shards sprayed at his feet in all directions where the crystal shattered, and a mark the color of blood began to spread over the rug. He spun around to see an elderly woman staring at him with her hands clasped in front of a starched white apron. Her jet-black hair had been slicked back into a tiny bun that seemed to pull against her skin at the temples, creating a concave depression where a pulse should be.

"Oh, dear. You've stained the Persian." Her voice was as crisp as her smock, and though her lips curled into a smile, her eyes remained dispassionate. She moved quickly for a woman of her age, which Patrick guessed must have been around eighty. "Step aside and I'll take care of that."

Patrick moved out of the way but kept his eyes glued to the old woman. She deftly pinched the shards with her fingertips and then dropped them into her open palm. After depositing each piece in the ash box near the fireplace, she blotted the rare Persian rug with ice. As if by magic, the ruby stain disappeared, and along with it, Patrick's hunger pangs. He offered a hand to her as she began to rise, which she gratefully accepted.

"My name is Patrick Don—"

"I know who you are, Mr. Donovan. We've been waiting for you." The woman stood with posture becoming royalty.

"We?"

"Thank you." She brushed the front of her apron with both hands. "Yes, those of us who work within the house have been aware of your pending arrival for quite some time.

"How…?"

She ignored the question and allowed her gaze to bounce around the room. "There are only a few of us to tend to the house, and when we have tenants, well… it's a bit challenging to accomplish everything in such a short time."

"I'm sorry, tenants? I don't understand. I thought this place was vacant." Patrick tossed a pitted date into the fireplace. "What did you say your name was?"

Her eyes darted from the fireplace to his face, and it was clear from her expression that she did not appreciate waste. "You should eat that which you select for yourself. Beggars are never choosy."

"I'm sorry. I just… was startled, I guess, and now I've lost my appetite."

"Pity." She folded her arms across her chest. "My name is Brienne Gillespie. You may call me Mrs. Gillespie."

Patrick cleared his throat. "Well, then, Mrs. Gillespie, would you mind showing me to my room? On the way, could you possibly point out the other help?"

She tossed him a cold stare but said nothing, nodded, and gestured to the entry foyer. Patrick walked ahead of her until they reached the vestibule, where he held back the curtain, waiting for her to pass. As if required, he said, "After you."

Mrs. Gillespie nodded her thanks and glided in. "Follow me." The stone lions seemed to watch Patrick as he moved past them and onto the stairway. "You needn't worry about the other 'help,' as you put it. You will see us up and about, now and then. Our duties are very defined, and we all work to keep the Sullivan House in order, as it should be." She had reached the first landing.

Patrick glanced overhead and saw at least three floors overhead. Each floor was encased in dark mahogany rails along the open hallways that disappeared into what must have been other wings.

"What's up there?"

Mrs. Gillespie said nothing but motioned for him to follow her down one of the hallways. He trailed behind, his eyes drifting along the numerous portraits that covered the walls. The faces, yellowing with time, were covered in dust. Gilded, hand-carved frames held each one securely to the wall. Patrick sensed that those who hung there detected his presence. He looked away, shivering.

"Who are these people?" he asked, hoping Mrs. Gillespie would answer this time.

"The masters of this house."

"All of these people? So many of them? They were the owners? Is that what you mean by 'master?'"

"This is a very old, well-established house, Mr. Donovan. Many have sought ownership of the estate, but few have mastered it."

The play on words was not lost on Patrick, but he was not going to aggravate the woman, either. He chalked her temperament up to isolation and old age. It was doubtful that Mrs. Gillespie knew much of the world Patrick had come from. In spite of her attitude, he would do the decent thing and cut her some slack.

He made a mental note: *Demand a little more respect, show them who the owner is now. Once I'm established, things will change. This isn't the 17th century, after all, and I expect some modern day courtesy, old age be damned.*

"At least there's electricity," he said instead. Instantly, he wished he hadn't—voicing a cover for his thoughts was a bad habit. He would need to check that in the future.

"Sometimes," Mrs. Gillespie replied. "We are secluded here, as you have noticed, and often fall back on the use of candlestick and flame for light."

She read my mind. Perhaps we'll get along, after all.

"That monk, back there. The one that met me at the door. Who is he?"

Mrs. Gillespie cleared her throat. "You'll see that the east wing is open in the morning, and the west, in the evening."

"You're not going to tell me, are you?" Patrick paused, but she gave no response. He tried another approach. "They haven't tried very hard to get those stains off the ceiling, have they?"

"Who, exactly, are you referring to, Mr. Donovan?"

"Someone… housekeepers, the help. Whoever it is that cleans up around here."

"Everyone that lives here volunteers to do so. There is no help, as you can see—only the residents."

Patrick dropped his gaze to the floor. She had a point—the upkeep to a mansion this size would be expensive. "I'm sorry. Of course, that makes sense. I've just never been in a place like this before."

"Yes, so it seems."

"Anyway, I didn't mean to be rude." He jogged ahead and stared at a painting of a woman, blindfolded and holding a juris scale. "I'm thinking of buying it, the house, you know. Be the new owner.

We'll get help around here—that'll be one of the first things we do."

"Of course."

They turned a corner and ascended a short stairway to a single corridor. The entry was flanked with heavy velvet draperies that had been pulled back to allow entrance—not that anyone walked there, anymore. The walls had been covered with flocked wallpaper in deep maroon and gold velvet. A solitary marble pillar supported a single bronze candelabrum with six tapers, unlit and waiting for use.

Just inside the dim ingress, a solitary doorway nearly eight feet in height came into view. The room beyond was sealed off by a set of mahogany double doors. A pair of cherubim had been carved into the center of each door, their innocent eyes staring blankly at anyone who might approach.

"Why is everything in here so dark?"

"As I said, Mr. Donovan, the Sullivan House is very old. The wood is aged, and the images carved therein have survived longer than the inhabitants who once dwelled here." She gently touched a cherubim's cheek and smiled, then pulled a large ring of keys from the pocket of her apron. Several skeleton keys jangled as she sorted through them. "This is your room."

"This one? It seems so far apart from the rest of the house. Isn't there one closer to the kitchen or something?" Patrick eyed the key as Mrs. Gillespie slipped it into the lock and turned it. The familiar click of tumblers sounded as they fell into place.

"This is the master's room. If you would prefer a guest room, instead…"

"No, no!" Patrick interrupted her. "I wasn't aware that this was the master suite. Where's my key?"

She lifted another key from her pocket and dropped it into Patrick's outstretched hand. Its weight was more than Patrick had expected. He glanced down the hallway—only darkness there.

"You are welcome to take mine if you'd prefer." Mrs. Gillespie held out the one she'd used to unlock the double doors. Patrick studied them both and saw that they were the same.

"No, thank you. I didn't realize keys were still made from… what is this, iron?" He turned the key over in his hand, feeling its weight against his palm. "Heavy."

"As I said, everything inside the Sullivan House is old, including the locks. It requires a sturdy key."

The shank was nearly three inches long, with a bit that stuck out in an L-shape at the bottom. Few 'teeth' had been cut into it, making Patrick question what type of security it provided. At the opposite end, a bow looped in tiny circles to form a cross, the center of which contained the image of a knight's helmet and letters he couldn't make out. The image was uncannily familiar. Patrick held it up for Mrs. Gillespie to look at. "Knights of Adrestia, huh? What? Do *they* have anything to do with this place?"

Mrs. Gillespie eyed the key for a moment, smiled, and then stepped through the narrow, yawning mahogany doors and into the dark chamber beyond, and whispered, "Not quite."

TWENTY

G HOSTS DANCED AGAINST THE WINDOWPANES, and Patrick stopped in his tracks when he saw them. Against two walls, they billowed in erratic movements inside the chamber. His breath caught and the thought *Run!* screamed in his mind. But Patrick could not. His feet were frozen in place and would not move. Instead, he waited—for what, he wasn't sure.

Decay assaulted his senses and he could barely breath due to the odor of it. Something scraped inside the darkness—the sound of a guillotine, or so Patrick thought. He began to tremble.

"No one has been in this room for a very long time, as you can see." Mrs. Gillespie's voice sounded from somewhere in the shadows. Patrick searched for her but saw only a skeleton-like figure peering from the hollow space next to the bed. It moved.

"Where... are you in...?" The words scratched against the back of his throat, sounding more like a whisper.

"I've opened the windows to let in some fresh air." The sound of the guillotine scraping followed her voice. Patrick turned, looking for the door he had entered through, but couldn't find it in the darkness. The urge to retreat overwhelmed him, but unseen hands held him inside the room, pushing him as if to force him farther inside.

Suddenly, a flame erupted from where the figure stood. It sputtered and then burnt steadily atop a taper that had been placed in a single candlestick. Unnatural streaks of light and shadow danced around the bedchamber, casting a ghoulish pallor to the face behind it. It smiled at him and began to walk toward him. A black mouth opened as the figure began to speak.

"You'll find that this room can be a very comfortable resting place, Mr. Donovan."

Patrick blinked and Mrs. Gillespie's face came into view, softening in the candlelight. She crossed to a small alcove and set the candle on a shelf set into the wall there. Then, returning to the darkness, she lit another match and brought a second taper to life. Its light illuminated the walls where the ghosts had been. Patrick saw that they were, in fact, sheer draperies billowing inward from the breeze through the opened windows.

"The guillotine," he whispered. *But they fluttered before the window was open.*

"I beg your pardon?"

"Nothing," he said and stepped forward. "I was just talking to myself about… about nothing."

Mrs. Gillespie smiled and nodded at him and then set the burning candle in a matching alcove on the opposite side of the room. Turning to her right, she opened a massive door and waved a hand toward the space inside. "Your bath."

"Where are the lights? Isn't there any electricity in here? I hope there's a TV somewhere. Don't want to miss football season." Patrick tried to chuckle. He dropped his duffle bag onto a tapestry bench that stretched the length of a carved footboard.

"There is no electricity in this wing, sir, except for in the bath. And there is no television. All of the other masters requested that outside interference be kept to a minimum in the sleeping chambers. Perhaps you feel differently than your predecessors from hundreds of years ago did?"

"No… I… it makes total sense. I was just joking about the TV, anyway. Why have cable or the internet or *lights* when you're trying to sleep, right?"

"I don't know what you mean, sir. There is an electric source in the bath for any hygienic needs you might…"

"I get it," Patrick interrupted. "So, what now?" He surveyed the room for a moment and then looked directly at Mrs. Gillespie. She had moved to the doorway without Patrick noticing and stood there, silently waiting for instructions. He shrugged. "What do people do after they arrive in houses like this?"

"Most choose to settle in and rest a bit. Supper will be served in the dining room at six. You can find the entrance from the same parlor that houses the damaged Persian rug." She smiled with dark eyes. "I will be happy to meet you there."

Patrick glanced at his watch and noted the time. "Six PM is in an hour. I guess I can keep myself busy 'til then."

"As you wish." She turned to leave.

"Oh," Patrick blurted out. "And stop blaming me for the rug. You startled me and it was a natural reflex. I'll buy another damn rug if you'll just stop talking about it."

"As you wish."

The door closed behind her and Patrick was left alone for the first time that day. He glanced from the bed to an ornate mahogany dresser. *You don't even have enough stuff to fill the drawers in that thing.* It was as if even the furnishings were trying to swallow him up. He was a tiny fly trapped inside a monstrous beast, a toy for the great house to play with.

He looked away and caught his own reflection in a mirror, jumped, and cursed again. Everywhere, eyes watched him—eyes that he could not find except in the reflection of the mirror.

"You've psyched yourself out, Pat. Freakin' calm down!"

He decided to freshen up. *Maybe that will help.*

Uneasy, he walked into the room attached to his bedchamber and probed along the wall, looking for a light switch. Finally, his fingers found the switch. He flicked it and a low display of bulbs flickered, then illuminated. Set into a line of antique lanterns mounted on either side of a full mirror, the bulbs looked out of place. It was obvious that these had been rigged only recently—the vestiges of tallow still aromatic as the bulbs heated old wax and iron.

"That can't be safe," Patrick said aloud, almost wishing the archaic lanterns hadn't been electrified. Fire seemed safer than electricity. He leaned forward across a basin sink and stared into the framed glass oval affixed to the wall as a bathroom mirror. His reflection looked odd in the beveled glass and he felt a bit unsettled, staring at it. His own image had startled him moments ago in the next room for almost the same reason.

"The estate can afford to pay for house help but cannot afford a decent mirror or electricity in the bedrooms? That's going to change. Let's hope there's running water." He turned the faucet handles and a stream of water spilled into the basin. "Well, that's big of them."

Patrick splashed cool liquid over his face and immediately felt better as the day's grime was washed from it. Looking up again, he stared at the mirror and saw a face that dripped with fatigue. Dark circles had formed underneath his eyes—a sure indication he needed sleep.

"Water can't wash that away," he said to his reflection in the mirror. "A good shower and that bed might, though." He laughed at his own ridiculousness and stared a moment longer, hoping the clock would chime six PM soon. He was hungry.

Then… he saw it.

A shadow behind him. Instead of just one—two faces stared back from the mirror.

TWENTY-ONE

"IT WAS A WOMAN, I'M telling you!" Patrick tried desperately to control his voice. "I saw her as clear as I see you."

Mrs. Gillespie folded her hands and waited for Patrick to calm himself. "I am sorry you've had a bad experience, Mr. Donovan. I suspect fatigue has gotten the best of you."

"Fatigue, my ass! There's someone in my room."

She shook her head. "That's impossible. Your room has been locked for nearly seventy-three years."

Patrick stared at her in disbelief. *The room has been vacant the entire time?* "I thought you said it was the master suite."

"Indeed, it is."

"What about the previous owner? Wasn't he, or she, the *master*?" Patrick couldn't hide the sarcasm in his voice.

"I think you are confused, Mr. Donovan. The house belongs to those who dwell herein."

"You're speaking in riddles again, Mrs. Gillespie, and I grow tired of trying to figure out what you're trying to say." He took a step back and glared at her. "Just who owns this house."

She smiled at him. "The original owner died a long time ago. Unfortunately, the deed was never transferred properly, so now, we're not really sure who owns it."

"But Wilkins said…"

"Mr. Wilkins has his opinion about it, as do many others. I'm sure you've heard the rumors."

"Oh, yes. I've heard the rumors. Treasure! That's what I've been told. Whoever owns… *owned* this place, apparently hid treasure inside, and I intend to find it. Find the deed too, while I'm at it."

Mrs. Gillespie lifted her chin and looked down at Patrick. "May I ask you a question?"

"Anything."

"Well, then, Mr. Donovan… what do you value most?" She held her hand up to silence the answer he was about to offer. "No need to respond. This is a question meant for your heart."

"Another riddle."

She smiled again. "Perhaps. But perhaps, I am simply asking you to reflect on your present situation. It just might be; the greatest treasure is the human soul. Have you considered finding that, Mr. Donovan?"

"My soul?" The word soured on his tongue.

She nodded. "Indeed. The worth of a soul is great in the eyes…"

"I know. I've heard it before—in church or something."

"Please let me finish. In the eyes of anyone who has lost his own—the worth of a soul is great. That, indeed, would be a treasure to someone left wanting, wouldn't it? And before you answer, please look around you. For nearly a hundred years, this magnificent house has been lacking a name, written officially on its deed. But, as you can tell, the Sullivan House does not go empty for want of souls."

Patrick was speechless. *There has been no one on the deed to this godforsaken house for nearly a century?* He opened his mouth but nothing came out. For the first time in a long time, Patrick was left speechless. He began to pace instead, pulling out his skeleton key and staring at it as he wore a path across the parlor's precious rug.

"What are you saying?" Finally, his voice had found him. "You mean to tell me not one single person has been in that room for over seventy years?"

She nodded and smiled with thin lips. "That is correct, Mr. Donovan."

"Then how did there come to be electricity in the bathroom and running water?" he snapped.

Mrs. Gillespie threw back her head, and a raspy sound that Patrick assumed was laughter escaped. The skin of her neck pulled tight and a scar that ran the length of it blanched. Patrick pulled his eyes from it as she looked down at him again.

"Why, Mr. Donovan, we installed facilities in the early fifties. This place…" She waved her hands outward and glanced at the ceiling. "…has always been fortunate to enjoy a more profitable, shall we say, circumstantial evolution, particularly with the import business. But, then, that is of no interest to you."

"Yes, it is! Absolutely!" he interrupted. "Tell me about this 'import business' after you explain how *no one* has been in my bedroom for seventy-three years."

"Come, we'll talk on our way to the dining room. There are others joining us for supper who can better answer your questions about the business of the Sullivan House." She began to walk toward the opposite end of the room where a large doorway joined the parlor to the dining hall. "This way."

"Tell me, who are these people joining us?"

Without responding, she continued to walk with her back to him. Patrick followed her across the lavish room that had once been a great meeting place, obviously used to smoke cigars, sip brandy, and share gossip.

"In regards to the electricity, it was decided to running water and electric power should be installed in the house sometime around the mid-1950s—a matter of convenience, really, although I question it." She cleared her throat. "The master's room was left without additional interference from modern utilities for the sole purpose of preserving its original state of peace." She swept her hand outward as they crossed the threshold into the dining room. "Ah, here we are."

Ahead, a vast table had been prepared with a full service of china and silver. Crystal goblets in various sizes topped each individual place setting and, off-center, two gold candelabras stood with tapers already lit. Underneath, set over a delicate doily of tea-stained lace, a silver platter contained ripe pears, apples, figs, and another fruit Patrick didn't recognize. Obviously, this would be a feast, and with nearly ten place settings ready, he would have company while he dined—as Mrs. Gillespie had mentioned.

"Who else? Business people?" Patrick motioned toward the table.

"Residents." She moved across the room to the doorway and greeted a slender woman as she entered. The woman kissed Mrs. Gillespie on both cheeks before turning toward the dining table. Patrick looked at her and thought she might have been attractive at one time in her life, but now appeared emaciated. *Drug addict*, he thought. *Wilkins warned me that this was used for rehab. I guess the 'residents' are going through detox or something.*

The woman took a place at the far end of the table and shifted her attention to a portrait hanging on the opposite wall. She didn't even appear to notice Patrick sitting there.

Freakin' messed up. Patrick looked away from her.

Another guest, followed by several more. None of them acknowledged Patrick, while each one affectionately greeted Mrs. Gillespie upon entering. Within moments, the great dining hall was filled with voices that spoke softly as if they were in a church. Most of those attending carried themselves well, as if trained in boarding school or a regal university. *Quite an interesting mix of characters going through rehab.* Patrick studied their faces—all gaunt, all addicts of some kind, he was certain.

"Well, you never really know who's hooked," Patrick said.

"What did you say?"

Patrick started, not realizing he'd voiced his thoughts aloud. Sitting next to him, a scrawny fellow fidgeted, rather rattled, or so it appeared. He shifted his position on top of the red velvet cushion of his chair. Patrick hadn't seen him sit, and was a little disturbed the bloke had been able to sneak up on him like that.

"Nothing," Patrick replied and moved his chair away a couple of inches. The guy stared at Patrick and chewed on the nub of a fingernail.

"Oh… because I thought I heard something come out of your mouth."

"Who are you?" Patrick grimaced as the man spit out a slice of fingernail onto the floor.

"Do you have a girlfriend? Is it Elisa?"

"What the hell?" Patrick stood and his chair clattered against the floor as it hit. "Who the hell are you?"

"Don't mind Phillip, Mr. Donovan. He means you no harm, do you, Phillip?" The voice carried a thick accent, foreign, from somewhere Patrick could not place. It came from the doorway. The monk entered—the same one Patrick had met earlier. Phillip shook his head.

"Dragon… my name's dragon," Phillip said, and began to chew on another finger.

"Of course it is," the monk said, and his smile was as placating as his tone.

"So, you do speak?" Patrick lifted his chair back into position without moving his eyes off the monk. "I don't like freaks… especially ones who call themselves 'Dragon.'"

"Mr. Donovan, surely you don't mean that. Phillip is a resident here and has paid his dues, just like everyone else." Several heads nodded in agreement. Patrick hadn't noticed the others that had taken their places—each person seated quietly, waiting for Patrick and the monk to join them.

Patrick stared at the gathering seated around the ornate table. Vacant faces stayed fixed on him, eyes boring through his soul as if that would somehow justify his seat next to an oddity named 'Dragon'. Patrick sat down. Then, slowly shifting his attention back to the monk, he asked, "Who are you?"

"Father Azrael Bielal. We met earlier. You may call me Father Azrael. Most do." The monk took the vacant place at the head of the table. Mrs. Gillespie sat at the opposite end and folded her hands.

"In my experience, the master of the house usually sits at the head."

"Yes, that is true. Are you dissatisfied with your place tonight?"

Patrick flinched at the question. *Best to leave it as is tonight, Pat. Tomorrow is a new day, as they'll soon find out. Still need to finalize the paperwork, or whatever needs to be done. Soon, Pat, you'll be the master here.*

Satisfied with his own justification, Patrick decided to change the subject. "I remember you. If I recall, you had very little to say to me." Patrick refused to look at anyone else, although he felt all eyes on him.

Father Azrael smiled again. "Indeed. Shall we begin? "He waved his hand in the sign of the cross, muttered something in Spanish or Latin, Patrick couldn't be certain, and lifted his goblet. "A toast." Everyone seated around the table lifted their goblets, as well, joining the toast from the monk at the end of the table. "To our newest arrival. Patrick. May your journey here amend the life you've lived outside of the walls of the Sullivan House."

Patrick stared at the monk. *A rather bizarre toast, but then, this whole place is bizarre. I'm definitely making some changes beginning tomorrow, after a decent night's sleep.* Patrick raised his glass in response.

"To Patrick." In unison, the voices floated his way from around the table.

"And to you all… my new associates. May the same be returned twice fold." Patrick smiled inwardly, containing the sarcasm behind his voice, and lifted the goblet to his lips. The deep burgundy liquid tasted richer than any wine he'd had before, and he closed his eyes to savor its flavor. "This is good."

"Only the best in this house."

The voice was delicate, feminine, and directly across from him. He snapped to and gazed at a young woman with ebony eyes and long lashes that fluttered when she blinked. She smiled at him and her dark skin glistened in the firelight as she lifted her own goblet in toast. Patrick watched as she sipped its contents rather provocatively. "They call me Caroline," she said, holding his gaze a little longer than was polite.

"Patrick."

"Come away from the fire, Mary. He isn't in there," Father Azrael called out. Patrick shifted his attention to the fireplace, ablaze at the opposite end of the room. A tiny woman stood at the hearth, staring into the flames. She was dressed in a plain linen shift that looked like something found in the attic of the house. In one hand, she clutched and crumpled the pale apron tied around her waist as if it were a lifeline.

"When did you light the fireplace? I don't remember any fire..." Patrick trailed off. He did remember feeling chilled as he walked into the room, but that sensation had passed, and while he still had goosebumps over his arms, he didn't feel the cold as intently any longer.

"Come, Mary. Take your place here with the rest of us." Father Azrael stood.

The woman looked at him, then glanced once more at the fire before walking to the only remaining chair at the table. She sat quickly but continued to look back at the blazing fire burning behind the grate.

"What's she so obsessed with anyway?" Patrick asked, and decided to take another nip at his wine. Alcohol would warm his bones, for certain, and likely dull his senses against the strange assembly at the table.

"Her newborn was burned alive in a fireplace."

Patrick started and turned to see a rotund man of about sixty standing with one arm draped over a marble bust, the other supporting a pipe. Smoke curled in slow motion around the crown of his head. He pointed to Mary with his pipe. "She's still looking for it."

"Will you be joining us this evening, Mr. Hunter?" Mrs. Gillespie's voice was laced with sugar.

The man with the pipe nodded. "After my smoke, sweet Brienne." He clamped the pipe between his teeth and puffed as color warmed Mrs. Gillespie's cheeks.

"She's sweet on him," a muscular woman sitting next to Caroline said. Her features contrasted with the flirtatious, dark-skinned beauty. This woman sat erect with her hands folded across the napkin in her lap. She stared askance at Patrick with pale blue eyes without turning her head. Patrick guessed the woman to be in her mid-fifties, although her mousy, wavy hair, pulled tightly in a bun at the back of her skull, made her look older. He couldn't be certain.

"That will do, Lizzie," Mrs. Gillespie said.

"Lizzie? Lizzie what?" Patrick gasped.

No one answered.

"Our meal chills." Father Azrael cleared his throat.

"Like the poem?" Patrick said. Lizzie cocked her head and her blue eyes turned to ice as she stared at Patrick. He assumed she hadn't heard the rhyme—perhaps she was indeed too old to remember it. "You know, 'Lizzie Borden took an axe and gave her mother forty whacks. When she saw what she had done, she gave her father forty–'"

"Stop!" Lizzie stood up from the table, a knife clutched in her hand. "Not true!"

"Whoa… I was just trying to play with you a little. No harm intended." Patrick pushed away from the table.

The man with the pipe chuckled, tapped the tobacco out into a tray, and walked to take his place next to Lizzie at the table. "She doesn't like that very much, do you, Lizzie?" Mr. Hunter put his hands on both of her shoulders and gently urged her back into her seat. "Hand me the knife now. This youngin' doesn't know Southern courtesy. It's our job to show him." The man with the pipe winked at Patrick.

"Thank you, Donald," Father Azrael said. He tossed a disapproving look at Patrick.

"It's Hunter," the big bloke said. His voice was crisp, as was his glare at the monk. "I do not use Donald any longer, as you well know, Father, and I would appreciate some respect for my name. Particularly as I don't address you as 'Bielal.'"

"My apologies, Hunter, I simply forgot." Father Azrael gave a simpering smile to Hunter, but his eyes burned red. Something sensitive had been said, and the monk felt its sting. "Now, I would like to get on with our meal, if possible, and let's stop this name-calling, shall we?"

"I, seriously, didn't mean any harm." Patrick glanced around the table for support. "She's obviously overreacting to a stupid child's rhyme."

"Let it alone," Caroline said. The smile was gone from her eyes, as well. Lizzie stared at her plate and Patrick mouthed *sorry* before draining his wine glass. He glanced at his own plate, heaped with steaming venison, roasted potatoes, and greens drizzled with butter. Cornbread and some type of twisted roll sat on the smaller plate to his left. Above the silverware, his wine glass rested, refilled to the brim with deep mahogany liquid.

"How…?" Patrick began but felt his throat constrict. He sat in silence and watched the others eating heartily. Silverware clattered and crystal sang as his companions chatted between bites. *I'm losing my mind,* Patrick thought as he speared a chunk of meat. *It's fatigue.* He realized he hadn't slept more than a few hours in the last forty-eight. *You need sleep. You need to eat too. Tomorrow you can sort this out.*

He placed the venison in his mouth and began to chew. Sage and one other flavor Patrick couldn't identify permeated the meat, and Patrick suddenly realized he was very hungry. He quickly stabbed another piece. "This is fabulous! My compliments to the chef," he said, waving a hunk of venison in mid-air just before plopping it into his mouth.

"Oh, that's Obediah's handiwork. He knows how to make a brilliant cut of venison, doesn't he?" Mrs. Gillespie sang out. The others nodded briefly and went back to their conversations.

Patrick grasped his goblet and lifted it. "To Obediah, then." Caroline tapped her goblet with her knife, and Hunter nodded, lifting his crystal in salute.

"To Obediah."

"I'm so grateful we can enjoy this meal together," Father Azrael said. "It's an honor to have you all here."

Another round of "Here-heres" and nods followed. Patrick lifted a forkful of potatoes into his mouth and glanced around the room. *Perhaps these people are just socially awkward.* He smiled at Hunter. *They are definitely hospitable, if nothing else.* Just then, he caught sight of a figure rushing by the doorway. It stood no more than three feet high had golden curls trailing down its back. It looked very much like someone he knew well—his daughter, Sarah. In a blink, she was gone.

And so were the others.

Patrick choked on something in his mouth. He looked at the empty places at the table. Cracked, ancient plates sat atop the table with decay heaped on top of them. Dropping his attention to his own plate, he saw piles of brown carcasses, and moldy mounds that housed maggots, crawling around inside. He gagged and pulled the last bite he'd taken from his mouth. A shriveled length of mash wriggled with the same tiny white bits of rice-looking insects. A maggot fell from the corner of his lips. Reaching for his goblet, he dumped the ruby liquid into his mouth, swished, and spat it onto the carpet. There was nothing there—no liquid, no wine, nothing. His mouth tasted of ash and he coughed against it.

"Bloody hell!" Patrick threw the goblet across the room. It shattered inside the cold, barren fireplace, splaying shards of glass against stone. "*What's going on here?*" Patrick shouted and ran for the doorway where he had seen the little girl. "Hey!" he shouted and looked for signs of anyone else in the house.

But there was no one—no one except Patrick and the whispers that floated in the silence of the Sullivan House.

TWENTY-TWO

"**B**E STILL, MR. DONOVAN. YOU'VE quite a bump on your head, I fear."

Patrick opened his eyes but the pain in his head screamed for him to shut them against the light. He did so, and waited for the ringing in his ears to stop.

"Oh, dear, he doesn't look good, does he now?" The voice was younger than the first, though both were female. Something cool was draped across his forehead. He felt it drip down his cheeks and run into both ears. Patrick hoped it was water and nothing more.

"I'm… I'm fine." Patrick tried to rise, but he hadn't the strength and fell back to the down pillow underneath his head.

"You don't look fine." A third voice had joined the others, her comments followed by a titteringed giggle. Patrick recognized the voice as the one belonging to Lizzy. He suddenly felt uneasy.

"Really, I'm fine," he said and forced his eyes open. "I don't need so many people fussing over me. I definitely don't need *her* in here." He eyed Lizzy.

Mrs. Gillespie whispered something in Lizzy's ear. She scowled at Patrick, turned on her heels, and walked out. Patrick took a deep breath and sighed.

"What happened?"

"Yer head."

Patrick looked to one side and saw Dragon standing in the corner, wringing his hands, the grin of a psychopath spreading across his face.

"My head?"

"Yup. Bleeding… right there." Dragon licked his lips.

Patrick reached for his scalp, felt the wet-sticky patch of hair, and winced. He pulled his fingers away and saw the tips were crimson. "How did this happen?"

"Don't play with it, silly." Caroline giggled.

Mrs. Gillespie placed a starched white towel over the place Patrick had fingered. "Hold this and put a little pressure on it, even if it hurts. That should stop the bleeding."

"*What the hell happened?*" Patrick sat upright but followed Mrs. Gillespie's instructions. "I don't understand. I was eating supper. You all were there. Then suddenly, you weren't and the table… maggots…" Patrick lowered his eyes, then remembering the little girl, he glanced at the doorway. "There was a little girl too. Right there." He pointed to the doorway.

Hunter tapped his pipe against the fireplace. Flames leapt, illuminating his face as he refilled the pipe. "You were knocked senseless. Hallucinating, likely. Kids aren't allowed in here."

"Maggots, either," Caroline said, laughing.

"She was right there. The fire was gone too. Suddenly, there was no fire in the fireplace and... ouch!" Patrick flinched as Mrs. Gillespie replaced the towel with another that had been saturated with something yellow and acrid-smelling.

"Hold still. This is rather nasty. I hope you don't have to visit the infirmary. That would be most unfortunate."

"There's an infirmary in this place?"

"Oh, no, Mr. Donovan." Mrs. Gillespie held out the soiled towel to Lizzy, who hovered in the hallway just out of sight. "Lizzy, please take this to Obediah. Perhaps he has more cerate. I fear we're running out."

"Indeed. The bees have not been as prolific this year," Hunter chimed in.

"Obediah is brilliant." Mrs. Gillespie patted Patrick reassuringly. "You've no worries. He will be able to cook up a very satisfactory cerate for this gash, even with the lack of beeswax this year." She shot Hunter a look, then turned back to Patrick and smiled. "You'll need to have this laundered anyway." She removed several bloody towels and held them out.

Lizzy walked in, snatched the soiled linen, and sneered at Patrick, then disappeared from the room and down the hallway toward the kitchen. Patrick eyed her as she left, then turned his attention to the others.

They watched him with broad grins. It was as if he were the main attraction at a carnival freak show, only the freaks were in the audience, staring down at him.

"I… I'm not sure I want that cerate stuff on my wounds."

"Relax, Patrick. Cerate is most efficient for treating flayed flesh." He heard a soft *tsk-tsk* coming from Mrs. Gillespie. "Lord knows, you were nearly scalped."

"Where's this infirmary? I need to see a doctor!" Patrick reached up to touch his scalp but decided he didn't want to feel it again. "This is bad. I need medical attention."

"What do you think we're giving you now?" Mrs. Gillespie cocked her head to one side, staring at him. Arguing would get him nowhere.

"I… I haven't felt well since I arrived here."

"Given your condition, that would make sense. But I would advise against it."

"Caroline! Hush!" Mrs. Gillespie shot her a dark look. "Phillip is still here…"

"Sorry, but it's my opinion. He asked and I think he should know. Dragon needs to deal with it, anyway." Caroline bent down and her voice turned spiteful. "It was a long time ago, Dragon. A long, long time ago. You should put it away in the past. Grow up a little… and for everyone's sake, stop that incessant rocking!"

"Caroline!"

Phillip had begun to rock back and forth. He stared, unblinking, off into the distance as his mind wandered somewhere else. With each prod from Caroline, Phillip rocked faster.

"Give the guy a break, Caroline," Hunter added.

Phillip began to tug at the base of his crown—his fingers filled with clumps of hair. Soft grunting sounds burbled from his throat. Patrick wondered if Dragon would vomit. He glanced at Caroline, who only laughed and folded her arms, watching him.

"I should know what? What are you talking about, Caroline? And where the hell is this infirmary?"

Caroline glanced up at Patrick and snickered.

"It's just that the Chandler Hospital has its skeletons—secrets, you know." Hunter puffed on his pipe as he spoke. "The place used to be the dumping ground for Yellow Fever. The tunnels, you know. It also housed the crazies…" He motioned to Phillip with the tip of his pipe.

"Mr. Hunter, really! That's not polite." Mrs. Gillespie stomped her foot and began to gather up emptied goblets and used linen. Patrick stared at her, his gaze darting to the table after a moment. There was a clean cloth spread out and set with fresh blooms in the center. All evidence of dinner service had been removed. Patrick shuddered.

"Used to be an asylum. Phillip knows it well, don't you, Phil?" Hunter chuckled, blowing out an O-shaped cloud of smoke.

"So, where's the damn infirmary, then? I'm not following any of you. This doesn't make any sense."

Patrick stood. Pain shot through his head and he felt woozy, but refused to give in to it. He placed a hand on the sideboard for support and noticed a silver bowl filed with fresh pears and nuts in the center. He shuddered again.

"The Yellow Fever struck, brought over on the ships carrying those damn religious zealots from across the ocean—Ireland or England or someplace over in Europe."

"Mr. Hunter! That will do!" Mrs. Gillespie stomped her foot, but he ignored her.

"The dock workers got it first. One by one, they'd disappear into the Chandler House. It had been set up as a makeshift hospital and never shifted back, except when it became a morgue. That was a bleak transition, if you ask me. I blame the Irish."

"No one has asked you anything, Hunter." Caroline sniffed and looked at Patrick.

"I'm asking and I'm Irish, so I have a right to know." Patrick shifted his weight.

"There you have it, Caroline. The Irishman is interested in history. He wants to know, so I'm tellin' the story, as I know it." Hunter nodded at Patrick. "As the fever set in, the bodies began to stack up. No one wanted a public panic, so it was decided that they would hide them."

As he listened, Patrick felt himself slip from the moment. Tightening his grip on the sideboard, he dug his fingernails into the palm of one hand to stay conscious. The sudden snap back to awareness made him wonder if consciousness was really a good idea. Hunter and Caroline continued sharing snippets of history, and something about their story made him feel uneasy. "The sick workers?" Patrick grimaced at the thought.

"The bodies. Most were dead the minute they hit the hospital, infected as they were. No place to put a ripe, diseased corpse. So, they piled them into the tunnels when the morgue filled up. Then, in the dark of night, gravediggers would sneak the bodies away and bury them before morning—most in unmarked graves."

Caroline smiled and her voice turned sugary. "They say the dead still wander there… in the tunnels."

"Right! You can't tell the living from the dead." Hunter chuckled and puffed another cloud of smoke.

Patrick glanced at the doorway. Lizzy had appeared again but hovered just outside, listening in. A twinkle flashed behind her dark eyes. *That woman is crazy! Everyone in this place is crazy! I've got to get out of here.*

Patrick moved toward the opposite side of the room. He looked for an escape but Lizzy prevented it. There was no doubt he needed to see a doctor. It was a good excuse. Somehow, he'd get medical attention, even if he had to walk to find it. Dropping his hand to his side, he felt the hard case of his cell phone.

Calling for help wasn't a solution since phone service wasn't available anywhere on the grounds. Dialing 9-1-1 was not an option. Possibly, he could flag down a passing car from the highway. Someone would see him eventually, maybe give him a ride to the nearest hospital—not the one with the underground tunnels.

"Thanks for the history lesson. I…I've got to go. I need help. This gash…"

"Hallucinating again." Hunter shook his head and stared at the fire.

"M-my head… it's too deep. I can't go much longer. I… won't see you later."

Caroline snickered again. "Probably will," she whispered and then clapped a hand over her mouth, stifling laughter.

Just then, Phillip stopped moving and slowly turned his focus on Patrick. "She didn't mean it. It was just her turn… her turn. She didn't think you'd make it. Her turn… her turn… her turn…"

Patrick froze. Everything cleared as his focus found Phillip. "What's he saying? Dragon, what are you saying!"

Phillip lifted his finger and pointed to the doorway on the opposite side of the room. A shadow hovered there, smiling with a twinkle behind her eyes. Clutched in one hand was an axe, its blade dripping blood onto the carpet. Patrick touched the wound in his scalp as Phillip repeated a familiar rhyme.

"Lizzy Borden took an axe.

Gave poor Patrick just one whack.

When she saw what she had done.

Someone told her, 'Better run.'"

TWENTY-THREE

NIGHT HAD FOUND ITS WAY to the Sullivan House, and with it, a dense fog that crawled with arachnid-like stealth, blanketing the surrounding estate so thickly that Patrick could not see his feet beneath him. He'd finally made it to the grounds and knew his car was parked not far from the front gate. If he could drive to get help, he'd return later for his belongings—including the deed to the Sullivan House.

He stumbled for the third time in just a few yards and slowed his pace even more. Obstacles hidden beneath the soupy fog tripped him—invisible hands clutching at his feet, it seemed—bruising his ankles with nearly every step. Patrick kept his eyes forward, afraid of what he might find should he look down. His thoughts brought visions of bodies hidden underneath the earth, buried in tunnels, grasping at anything aboveground—even his heels.

Perhaps there are tunnels under the Sullivan House too.

Patrick shook the thought away and pushed forward to a break in the tree line. *Surely, that's a way out of here.* But the trees only seemed to move together, forming an alcove that protected a set of marble cherubim. Each held a vase, long dried-out and empty of water.

A fountain. Damn!

He turned back and faced the only reference point visible in the fog—the Sullivan House. It stood taller than he remembered. White ossein stone walls had been darkened by algae and soot. The windows blinked a yellow, sickly glow, and Patrick thought of the bodies trapped in the tunnels again.

Time to move—get out of the alcove and find another exit. The road has to be near here. I parked my car just in front... there.

Nothing but fog.

Patrick drew a visual line from the massive front doors to where his car should be. Bubbling vapor stretched to the edge of another line of trees. It was as if the entire estate had been cut off from civilization and everything along with it had disappeared.

He pulled his cell phone from his pocket and glanced at the screen. No bars, no service. Patrick dialed 9-1-1 anyway and prayed the call would go through.

"We're sorry. Your call cannot be completed at this time." Three ascending tones followed. *"We're sorry. Your call cannot be completed at this time."* Three tones again. *"We're sorry. Your call—"*

Patrick tapped the phone off and scanned the perimeter of the grounds again.

"It's got to be there… somewhere," he said to no one, and traced his steps back to the front of the house again. Turning his back on the massive front door, he began to walk straight ahead. "The car is there. Right in front. I just can't see it… or anything else, for that matter. Damn fog! You'd think I was in Iberia."

A few paces farther on, Patrick reached out for the gate that had been there when he'd arrived. Nothing but empty space. He watched his hand disappear into the dense vapor and wondered if invisible hands would grasp at his fingers, as well. Something stabbed at his ankle and he jumped aside. Patrick winced and rubbed his ankle, then took a few more steps.

"It's got to be here. The damn iron spikes stood taller than my head. They've got to be."

The gate wasn't there.

Patrick wandered to the edge of another tree line. He pushed against them, but the trunks were no more than a few inches apart. He followed the wall of trees for a while, hoping to find an opening, but there was none. Branches angled in distorted arms, forming a barricade.

To keep strangers out… or, perhaps, to trap others inside.

Patrick's ankle burned. He could not see anything below his knees and could only guess as to its severity. Another injury would slow his progress and make for a long night. "The medical staff will be busy with me, if I can only get out of…"

Something growled.

The sound came from his right. He turned to see where it had come from and saw nothing but the dense mist. Slowly, Patrick began to retrace his steps. Keeping his eyes focused in the direction of the noise, he began to step backward, aiming for the only landmark visible—the Sullivan House.

The growl sounded again, this time a pitch higher, as if the creature's throat was constricting. Patrick's spine crawled. Whatever made the sound, the noise had the same effect as fingernails being dragged the length of a chalkboard.

Disoriented, Patrick looked to the Sullivan House to get his bearings. It had moved—suddenly far off in the distance. Had he travelled that far? It wasn't possible. Patrick's skin prickled and he felt the hair on the back of his neck rise.

Another growl sounded from behind.

There's more than one. Patrick's focus snapped to the trees. Something stood in there, watching, waiting. Unblinking, rubescent eyes stared through the thicket for a just moment before suddenly dropping below the fog. *They're tracking you, Patrick. Whatever they are, they're hunting as a pack, trying to drive you farther away from the house—farther away from safety.* The thought struck him as odd. How could the Sullivan House be a place of safety? Wilkins had called it a place of refuge once, but Patrick hadn't understood what that meant, not then.

He did now.

Patrick doubled back, carefully placing each step so as not to fall. That would surely mean the end of him, and the beginning of a gory meal for whatever hunted him beneath the fog's cover. "Keep it together, Pat," he whispered for his own sake. His head still throbbed, and the slow movement of the vapor was making him feel dizzy again.

Another growl, closer this time, was followed by the searing pain of flesh being torn from his calf. His knees gave way and he felt himself fall. Patrick's reflexes kicked in as his hand reached out, bracing for the fall. Instead, it disappeared beneath the vapor and landed on something coarse, hairy, and solid. He cried out, mostly from fear, but the pain in his leg tore at him again—a reminder that something was eating him.

Another snarl, and the same fiery pain shot up his arm. He retreated, caught his balance, and began to run. This time, he cared little about his footing, only that he needed to get away.

"Help me!"

Patrick ran, stumbling again and again, but never falling completely to the ground—that would be certain death. The crimson eyes had doubled in number, each beast circling him as he ran. He couldn't make out exactly what the creatures looked like, but Patrick knew they were many.

Something snarled and leapt out of the mist, snapping wildly at one side. Patrick shifted direction and the animal disappeared into the fog. *That was too close.* Patrick recoiled, turning the opposite way with his full weight on his injured leg. Crying out, he forced himself to put weight on it. Fortunately, adrenaline kept him from noticing much more than the predators below the fog. His leg would have to bear him up a little longer.

He still hadn't seen the damage, but he could smell blood—his own blood—and he knew the creatures chasing him could too. He scanned the sea of fog that seemed to be growing denser as he ran.

No landmarks. No way to know where he ran, but Patrick knew he couldn't stop. Ahead, he saw the Sullivan House. The only object looming above the vapor—the house that wanted to consume him too, just as the beasts attempted to devour his flesh.

Patrick screamed for help again.

The front door swung open, and inside, a single light flickered—a beacon in the darkness, bidding him to run to the house—to safety.

"Oh, please, let me make it…" It was the first prayer Patrick had uttered in many years. Perhaps something had heard it.

The door yawned wider.

Suddenly, a high-pitched whistle sounded in the distance. Immediately, the growling stopped and the beasts retreated. Patrick saw the red eyes disappearing as he threw himself onto the front porch stairway. Lapping at the base, the fog beckoned him to return. Patrick scrambled to the top of the porch, collapsing with exhaustion and something else. As he lay there, the warmth of sticky liquid collected beneath his body and stirred his senses.

"No… oh, God, *no!*"

Patrick rolled over, staring at threads of muscle and sinew hanging from white matter where his lower leg had been. Below, a solitary set of bones joined his knee and foot. Patrick shrieked and reached for the meaty bones—but there was nothing there. His hand was gone. The bloody stump of an arm wagged, instead.

Then, everything went black.

Behind him, the Sullivan House welcomed him in… again.

TWENTY-FOUR

"**O**PEN YOUR EYES. DO IT!"

The voices sounded as if they were being shouted from a tunnel far away. The words battled with an incessant buzzing inside his head, distorting reality into a nightmare.

"He can't hear you. He's still out cold. Give him a minute."

"Open your eyes, Patrick!"

He struggled to do as he had been told, but Patrick's sight remained dark. He turned his head slightly, hoping to hear what they were saying in the tunnel. Maybe the ringing and buzzing would stop and he would wake.

"See that! I saw him move. Snap out of it, Patrick. You're being a sissy about all of this!"

The sharp sting of a hand slapping his face brought him to, and Patrick opened his eyes.

"He hears you. He does. Sees you now too." This time from a male voice, nervous, and high-pitched.

Another sting, this time to the other cheek, brought indignation. "Stop it!" Patrick's voice sounded weak, but the message was clear. He blinked and light registered shapes, enough to make out triplicate faces only inches away. All three stared down at him. Lizzy's hand was raised for the next slap. Patrick snatched it, holding her by the wrist. "I said *stop* it!"

"You're right, Dragon. I think he's fully awake now." Caroline smiled and turned her attention to the foot of the settee where he lay. "This may sting a bit, now that you're conscious. But Mrs. Gillespie said to keep the tincture on and change the bandages every hour. Take a deep breath. Here we go."

Fire shot from the front of Patrick's leg to his armpit. He arched and cried out. Several pairs of hands held him down as he flailed.

"Let go of me, you pathetic waste!"

Lizzy twisted against the grip Patrick had on her wrist. Pain shot through his leg again and Caroline wrapped the dressing taut. He gripped Lizzy's wrist tighter.

Then he remembered. *Fog. Creatures. A bone for a leg. And my hand.*

Patrick looked for his mangled arm. He saw two hands with fingers—each attached to his perfectly intact arms. One of his hands was clenched in a vice-like grip on Lizzy's wrist. He loosened it and stared at his appendage as he turned it back and forth. The knuckles were raw and bleeding, as was his palm, but it was there. A tiny line ran the circumference of his wrist. He squinted at it, then remembered another that was just the same. Glancing up at Caroline, he looked at the same line around her neck.

Quickly sensing his interest, she placed a hand to her throat, covering all traces of the mark. Darkness flashed behind her eyes. Something about that mark was not welcomed fodder for a stranger's eyes. Patrick forced his attention back to his injuries.

"My hand! It was bitten off. There was no…" Patrick remembered his leg. He sat upright and peeled the dressings off his lower leg. Beneath, the skin was intact, though gashes and ruddy abrasions ran the entire length of his shin.

Caroline sighed. "Now we have to start over. Thanks a lot, Patrick."

"My hand! Leg!" He touched his scalp and felt the scab that ran along it. "And my head!" Scanning their faces, Patrick looked for Lizzy.

She had moved aside and stood next to the tiny fireplace set between the bookcases that ran the length of the Cherrywood paneling. Beside her, Hunter spun a world globe balanced on a simple wood platform and cocked his head, listening intently to Lizzy's whispering. Occasionally, they'd all glance at Patrick before shifting their focus to some other adornment in the cozy library.

"Ah, Mr. Donovan. I see you're with us again." Mrs. Gillespie's voice sounded cheery as she entered the room.

"Not willingly," Caroline muttered as she placed a new bandage over Patrick's leg. "If Dragon hadn't pulled him up the stairs, he'd likely have fallen back down them again, and who knows what he'd have done to himself? As it is, I can barely get him to hold still long enough to let me put these…" She held up another readied bandage. "…where they'll do any good."

Patrick glanced down at Hunter's stovepipe boots. Bits of grass and mud stuck out from the base of the leather soles. A scattered sheen over his trousers suggested he'd been outside in the weather.

Patrick's jaw clenched. "Do you like to hunt, Hunter?"

"Hunter. It's his name. There's a reason." Dragon laughed and shifted from one foot to the other.

"Nickname, actually. My given is forgotten." He cleared his throat and stood tall.

"No, it's not. It's Donald Taylor. But that's a bad name. Too many people know that name, so he's now called Hunter, because that's what he does best." Dragon began to hop from one foot to the other, singing, "'Hunter went a-hunting, but the bird got away.'"

Patrick leveled a dark stare at Hunter. It helped to distract him from the sting in his leg where Caroline had placed the next bandage. He studied the man called "Hunter." Glinting in the firelight, a silver whistle dangled from his neck and hung nearly to Hunter's belt. It swung like a pendulum as he spun the globe again.

Steeling his look, Patrick locked eyes with the man in boots. "And do you hunt with dogs, perhaps, *Hunter*?" Patrick bit off each syllable.

Hunter turned his back and faced the fire. "I'm not answering these questions. Give him something so he'll shut up. His clumsiness has caused enough injury to make the man delirious."

"True… true. People who hurt their heads go mad. People who go mad need medicine to be good again," Dragon said. His speech had slowed in time with his hopping.

"Well, you should know, Dragon. You're crazy as a loon!" Lizzy snapped. "I've had quite enough fun for one day. Please excuse me." Without waiting for a response, Lizzy disappeared through the door.

"I'm finished here, as well. I've got some cleaning up to do. Today turned out rather poorly, and I'm not in the mood for social discourses this evening. *Adieu*." Hunter bowed, then followed Lizzy out the door, headed in the opposite direction from her.

"That's interesting, don't you think? His boots were covered in mud and he had a dog whistle around his neck."

"How do you mean, Patrick?" Mrs. Gillespie's voice sounded flat.

"I mean, I was nearly eaten by creatures outside this wretched house and *Hunter*… that stiff, Donald Taylor, or whatever his name is, looks exactly like he's gone hunting—with *dogs*, nonetheless!"

"I don't see why you're getting so worked up."

"Don't you see? The guy fed me to his dogs!" Patrick gestured to his leg.

"You fell down the front porch stairs, Mr. Donovan. Dragon found you and helped you back into the house. I really think you owe him a kind word along with your pending gratitude." Mrs. Gillespie nodded to Phillip while keeping her attention focused on Patrick.

"Thanks," was all he could muster.

"You seem to have issues with some of our residents. It appears Mr. Hunter and Lizzy bring you concern every time you're in their presence. Why is that?"

"I… they…" Patrick had no explanation that made sense, even in his own mind. At least they had gone away. The night would be more peaceful without the two of them.

Patrick sighed. Mrs. Gillespie would never understand, and his head still hurt. He glanced at the others staring at him. Once he'd recovered from his wounds, he would deal with each of them separately. He stared at Phillip, who was rocking in place with the same psychotic grin spread over his face.

As silly as Dragon seemed, he had logic behind his words—head injuries did often preclude an alteration in consciousness. Patrick had learned that sad fact the day his little girl, Sarah, had rolled down a flight of stairs in her walker. She was barely a year old and just starting to walk. They'd spent the entire evening in the Emergency Room, getting cat scans and X-rays while the nurses kept them company, mostly for observation. The memory wrenched Patrick's gut—he had been responsible for watching Sarah that day.

"I don't understand how all of these things keep happening to me. How did I get in here? Where is this… this library, or whatever it is?" Patrick said, trying to distract his thoughts.

"This *is* one of the house's many libraries—the smallest one, actually. Dragon heard you screaming. He found you crawling up the front porch stairway. When you finally made it to the top, you collapsed and hit your arm and leg on the edge of the iron railing. It's a miracle you didn't break anything." Mrs. Gillespie shook her head and made a clicking sound with her tongue that reminded Patrick of his own mother's *tsking* when she was displeased.

"Probably a mild concussion from the whack on your head." Caroline folded her arms and inspected the dressings on his leg from where she stood. "If you'll leave these alone, you should heal up fine. Fuss with them, and it's not my problem."

"Who whacked me over the head?"

Mrs. Gillespie looked at him askance. "Caroline didn't imply anyone had whacked you over the head. She simply meant that you whacked your head on something, didn't you, Caroline?"

"Of course. You're hearing things, Patrick."

Patrick stood, his indignation getting the best of him. "I know what I heard. You said I was whacked over the head, like the rhyme, 'Lizzy Borden took an axe, gave her mother forty whacks.' Even Dragon said it. I saw it too. Earlier, I saw her holding something bloody in her hand… a knife or a hatchet or something. It fits, doesn't it? Lizzy… Lizzy! That's who she is, isn't she? Only, *that* Lizzy is dead!"

Mrs. Gillespie moved quickly. Placing her hands on his shoulders, she urged him to lie back down. "Mr. Donovan, you're working yourself into a dither."

"I know what I saw!" He shrugged her off. "Just now, I was chased by some kind of creature… a pack of them… with red eyes that ripped into my leg and chewed off my hand." He held up his hand and stared at the line about his wrist. "It's been sewn back on or something. My leg too. All the skin was off and only the bone—"

"It's the head injury." Mrs. Gillespie directed her comments to Dragon. "Help me get him down, and you…" She looked up at Caroline. "Mr. Hunter was right. He needs something now. We cannot wait until later, as scheduled. Do your best, dear."

In a single leap, Dragon was on Patrick, pinning him to the settee with one knee while he held both arms fast with strength unbecoming his wiry frame. He stared down at Patrick with wild eyes. Patrick tried to pull free, but could not move.

So strong for such a scrawny piece of shit!

"Now hold still, Mr. Donovan." Mrs. Gillespie's voice had turned.

"You'd best open your mouth and do as you're told or we'll be pressed to force it down you," Caroline chimed in.

"Get off me! No! Stop it!" Patrick's cries went unheeded.

Caroline stepped up, holding a teacup in hand. "Drink this. You'll feel better. It's really the easiest way, trust me."

"I'm not drinking anything! You're trying to poison me!"

Caroline's face blanched and she exchanged looks with Mrs. Gillespie, who nodded. "Pinch his nose if you must."

Patrick pressed his lips tightly together and twisted his head from side to side. Bony fingers clamped his nostrils together. Patrick couldn't breathe.

They're trying to kill me!

Gasping, he opened his mouth. Bitter, warm liquid ran into his mouth and he nearly choked. He tried to spit it out, but a hand quickly clamped his jaw shut. There was nothing he could do but swallow. It burned his throat and he felt an immediate urge to vomit.

Patrick smelled the blood before he tasted it. The hand moved away and he felt his limbs stiffen. Arching again, he exhaled blood from his nose, matching the froth that spewed from his mouth. Suddenly, every muscle constricted and he felt his body spasm.

"Relax, Patrick. That will all go away in a minute. Then you'll rest peacefully." Caroline's voice trailed off like an echo, and for Patrick, the world went dark for the second time that day.

TWENTY-FIVE

When Patrick opened his eyes, the room seemed to expand. From a cathedral ceiling, a single chandelier hung mid-chamber. Each of its thirteen sconces burned tallow candles that sent black smoke overhead. Netting draped the entire bed frame where he lay. Beneath, the linen felt damp. Though soft, the mattress was a reminder that Patrick's body ached.

Patrick rolled uncomfortably to one side and pushed himself up to rest on one elbow. Across from the bed, the oversized, elaborate mirror reflected a stranger trapped inside a gauze shroud. He stared for a moment, startled at the face that stared back. With effort, Patrick moved aside the linen and climbed out of the bed, shuffling his way to the mirror for a better look.

"Something's wrong," Patrick said under his breath, moving closer to the glass. Dust was layered over the surface, creating distortion to the images he saw there, including his own. "What the hell?"

Patrick leaned in closer and ran a finger along the side of his face. The stranger did the same. Grotesque features looked Patrick in the eye, blinking at the same time as he did. Its hair was matted on one side, caked in something shiny and hard. The mouth opened and closed in the same sequence when Patrick spoke. It had cracked black lips pulled tight across skeletal teeth, broken and grey. Dull, glazed-over eyes stared back, surrounded by dark circles that framed dry orbs with no focus.

"A dead man's eyes."

The vision mouthed the words as Patrick said them. He reached a hand to his scalp and saw only a meaty stump where a wrist should be. Nothing was attached to the limb that had withered against the bone.

Patrick gasped and stumbled backward, crashing into a tea table long forgotten and dusted with webs. Silver and porcelain shattered on the stone floor, sending a horrible noise that echoed over and over within the rafters. Patrick covered his ears.

"Stop it!"

He glanced around the room and saw that the candles were dark. Dust and stone framed the dungeon that held him captive. Except for the bed and a single chair, the room was vacant. He recognized it at once. This was his room—the master's suite, as Mrs. Gillespie had called it.

Patrick rushed to the door. It was locked. He pounded on it, screaming for someone to let him out. No one responded, and he heard no noise from outside.

Patrick ran to the overturned cart, snatched it, and threw it against the door. *That will bring someone… anyone. Dragon, at least.*

Nothing.

He ran to the bathroom, avoiding the mirror as he searched for anything to pry the lock open. Behind the dressing table, he found a steel snuffer, used to put out the flames of burning candles. It was small and felt a little brittle in his hands, but it would have to do. Running back into the main room, Patrick froze.

The door was open wide.

"Hello?" He crept toward it, looking into the hallway for signs of life, but all he saw was darkness. "Anyone there?"

"I'm right here. Cleaning up the mess you made with the tea service. Did you not notice it when you awoke? I suppose you didn't."

Patrick jumped and turned to see Mrs. Gillespie on her hands and knees, picking up pieces of broken porcelain and righting the overturned silver pot. It gleamed as she wiped it dry, then blotted the rug where another stain had set in.

"I didn't hear you come in."

"You certainly have a propensity for damaging our fine tapestry. Why is that, Mr. Donovan?"

Patrick could hear irritation in her voice. "I'm sorry. I didn't mean to. It's just that the mirror…"

"Tell me you haven't damaged the mirror, as well." She stood and walked over to inspect the glistening glass. Patrick caught his own reflection and saw his face looking back. The layer of dust was gone, as was the fiend that resided in the mirror. Only he and Mrs. Gillespie were reflected there. Patrick felt his gut wrench. *I don't know what's worse—the corpse that stared back at me or my own reflection!*

"The mirror… it was dirty and distorted. A face in the glass that…" Patrick trailed off. "Never mind."

"We tend to see what we desire, Mr. Donovan. What is reflected back is not always reality." Mrs. Gillespie smiled and wiped her hands on her apron. "Well, I'll be leaving you to rest. You've had quite a busy few days here."

"Has it been that long? How many days?"

"Oh, I don't know for certain, Mr. Donovan. I have little use for calendars anymore." She walked out of the room, pausing with her hand on the door handle. "Shall I close this for you?"

"No!" Patrick cleared his throat. "No, thank you. I'd prefer it remain open for a while."

She smiled at him. "As you wish." Then, Mrs. Gillespie disappeared into the darkness of the hallway.

Patrick stared at the empty space for a moment, fear creeping into his veins as he realized he was once again alone. "Maybe this isn't a good idea, after all. I don't even know who owns the Sullivan House. Probably out of my budget, anyway. Definitely a fix-er-upper with lousy tenants."

He walked to the bathroom and turned on the hot water faucet. Steam immediately rose, filling the bathroom. Patrick started. *Not that. Not fog!* He turned the other faucet and waited for the cold water. Out of habit, he glanced up at the mirror, then realizing his mistake, turned away.

Out of the corner of his eye, he spotted the shadow of someone hiding behind the bedroom door. Slowly, he stood, forgetting the water as it gushed into the sink, and walked into the bedroom. The shadow darted to the open door, disappearing into the hallway.

"Enough of this! Who's there?" Patrick's voice betrayed his fear. He cleared his throat and spoke again, this time a little more sternly. "I demand to know who's there!" He stopped at the doorway and stared into the darkness.

"Daddy?"

The voice was but a whisper. Patrick peered down one direction and then the other, but found nothing on either side.

"Daddy."

The voice sounded to his right, a little louder this time. Patrick stepped into the hallway and faced the long corridor. Cloudy windows ran the length of the exterior wall, with sheer draperies billowing in an invisible breeze. He could just make out the shape of a little girl—the same apparition with golden curls and a spectral voice.

"Sarah?" Patrick cocked his head and took a tentative step toward the ghost.

"Daddy. Why?" The voice trailed off, a whisper, barely a breath of something that lived once and now remained only as a memory.

Patrick wondered if his mind was playing tricks on him again, or if this was real—his daughter, his Sarah. It moved, and a wake of shadow and haze was left for Patrick to follow. Outside, the skies flashed as another aberrant bolt of lightning snaked a little too close to the house. As if lighting his way, the entire hallway blazed and the apparition darted into a darkened room.

"You're afraid of the dark, Sarah. You're afraid of storms too, I remember."

Patrick followed her down the hallway as another burst of lightning sent the hairs of his arm on end. He picked up his pace and the sheers waved an ethereal "goodbye" behind him. When he'd reached the doorway, he stopped. The prickling of his arms had nothing to do with the lightning.

"Daddy."

The apparition stood just inside, waiting for him. She stared with wide eyes, blonde curls blowing in an invisible breeze. Her pale skin showed none of the rosy glow Patrick remembered in his daughter's cheeks.

"Sarah. Come with me."

Her ghostly expression looked sad as she shook her head. *"You can never leave."*

"Of course I can. Come with me. Let's go some-where where we can be together." He held his hand out to her.

She said nothing, only stared at him, and Patrick felt a chill. This was his daughter, and yet, it wasn't. He had never felt fear in little Sarah's presence, but now…

"*You can't leave here.*" She raised her arm and pointed to something across the room.

"I'm not going in there, Sarah. It's dark… secretive. You shouldn't be in there, either. Come with me. Let's get out of here, just you and me. This is a bad place, sweetie. Gives me the creeps."

"*You can never leave.*" She pointed again and Patrick looked.

Standing by the farthest wall, the woman he'd seen before stared at a massive bookcase, her back turned to him. He recognized her instantly. "Heather!"

She turned to face him. Her features moved as if every molecule was trapped in time--from another dimension. A pale vapor haloed her, and Patrick felt ice in his veins. She smiled but there was sadness in her eyes, as well. Sarah floated across the room to join her mother and both stared at him again with the same wide-eyed sorrow.

"Heather, come with me."

"*This is not an illusion, Patrick. You belong here now.*" Heather's voice, wispy and distant, brought Patrick to his knees.

He clasped both hands in front of him, praying as if he faced a deity, but he knew this was far from it. Glancing around the massive library, he hoped to find something to bring him hope—a Bible, perhaps—but there was none. Only dusty books that climbed nearly forty feet of oak shelves.

"Help me, Heather. What is this place?"

"*A place of retribution.*"

He swallowed against a dry throat and felt himself struggling to breathe. "Retribution for what?"

Overhead, an immense chandelier began to sway. To one side, an iron spiral staircase quaked and books fell from their forgotten places. The spirits stared at him with vacant eyes.

They'd give him no comfort.

Patrick glanced at the room that seemed to be collapsing in around him. *The Sullivan House wants to destroy me.* Without blinking, Patrick felt tears stain his cheeks. He looked back at what had once been his wife and daughter.

"*Daddy, why?*"

He reached out to them. "Oh, baby girl. I don't know. I'm trying to understand." Looking to the woman, he cried out, "From what, Heather? Retribution from what?"

She stared at him and he heard something whisper.

"From sin."

TWENTY-SIX

ANOTHER BOLT OF LIGHTNING SHOOK the library and books flew from the shelves, catapulted against one another, aimed at nothing in particular—a violent display of invisible force that wanted Patrick. He ducked and covered his head as if that would do any good against the entity. When he looked up again, the apparitions were gone.

He was alone in a room that wanted to consume him.

"What do you want from me!" he screamed, shaking his fists. "I'm the victim here! I paid retribution every day they interrogated me—no wait, *humiliated and harassed* me—in that damn courtroom. I've already paid my dues!"

"You have only begun, Mr. Donovan."

Patrick spun around to see Father Bielal standing in the doorway. His robes hung undisturbed by the chaos erupting inside the library. Patrick, still on his knees, looked at the priest as the raging room tore at him mercilessly. "Help me."

"That is why I am here, my son." Father Bielal stepped across the threshold and instantly, the room fell quiet. Patrick collapsed, catching himself with both hands, or so he thought.

Seconds later, the floor rose up, smashing his nose against the hardwood. He rolled to his back as blood spewed from both nostrils. Patrick reached up to stop the bleeding and stared at the space where his hand had been.

"Oh, hell no! Not this!" Patrick crawled across the room to a chair, pulled himself to his feet using his only hand, and limped to the window. Without looking at it, he knew only bone supported the weight of his body—his leg missing the meaty part of its flesh, consumed by beasts not long ago.

Another bolt of lightning blinded him for just a moment before the glass turned black again. There, he saw the reflection of the carcass he'd seen before. He lifted his arm and stared at the withered stump. Pieces of bone poked through, less shiny this time. Decay had set in and Patrick could smell it.

"When fate's mirror reflects the truth, we never like what we see. Reality, as you notice, Mr. Donovan, isn't always as we wish it to be." Father Bielal stood statuesque with hands clasped and hidden inside his robes' sleeves. As if it would matter, Patrick desperately wanted to see them—to see if perhaps the monk's hands were decayed, as well. But he knew it wasn't true—the priest's face was clean, with an unusual porcelain cast.

"I don't know what kind of mind game you're playing here, Bielal, but I'm not falling for it. You have a goldmine in this house and you're all trying to protect it." Patrick's gut wrenched. "You and your cronies drugged the wine or something. Don't want me buyin' this place, and you're trying to scare me away. Well, it won't work! I don't scare that easy, I'm tellin' ya!"

Patrick pushed past Father Bielal and strode into the hallway.

"Indeed, you've still much to learn, Mr. Donovan."

The entire house remained in darkness, but Patrick didn't need a light to see anymore. He knew exactly where he was going, and no one would stop or distract him this time. He turned to his right and headed down an unfamiliar passageway, ignoring the stare boring into his back from the library.

"You can go to hell, priest!" He turned a corner and disappeared.

"Much to learn…" echoed behind him.

*****

Deep within the house, an air of obscurity seeped everywhere that Patrick strode. Nothing looked familiar—he'd obviously never been this far into the bowels of the Sullivan House before, not that it mattered. So much needed to be explored anyway, and likely, the money or gold or whatever the treasure hidden here would be buried deep within uninviting corridors or in an abandoned wing.

He set his resolve and spotted the flicker of something in the distance. "There is life down this way, after all," he said as he made for the flickering light.

It sparked bluish against the next lightning flash— almost as if the light from inside reached out to grasp hold of the other.

"Good. We need better lighting in this place. Light it up, thunderhead. Impress me!"

As if in response, several blinding bolts lit up the estate, haloing skeletal trees and the gargoyles set atop their posts throughout the grounds. Patrick threw his head back and shrieked wildly, laughing, "Is that the best you can do? Weak! Timid weakling!"

"Don't mock the squall."

Patrick jumped. "Dragon! What are you doing down here?"

"My papa told me to never mock the squall!" Dragons' hands balled into fists. "Never… ever mock…"

"I'm sorry, Phillip. I've never been told that before." Patrick glanced from his face to his fists.

The man they called Dragon looked harmless, but Patrick had seen rage like that before, and Phillip could barely contain his. Who knew what damage the wiry psycho could do if angered enough. Maybe that's where his nickname came from.

"Look, no harm meant, okay? Relax and take a breath. I… I'm here to…" In truth, Patrick didn't know where he was or why he stood, shouting at a thunderstorm inside the house. It wasn't like him to act so brash, and yet, he had been reckless before—the very act that had brought him to the Sullivan House in the first place.

Phillip said something but Patrick didn't hear the words. *Better to distract a crazy man than let him go off.*

"Isn't this a magnificent storm?" Patrick pointed to the window with his stump. *Odd that Phillip doesn't notice.* Patrick ignored his own disgust at the decaying flesh and forced a smile.

"Yes."

"Let's watch it together. I was just looking for a good place to sit and watch. Maybe you know of a good place. I'll bet you do, don't you, Dragon? Someplace we can watch the lightning together."

Phillip smiled and nodded his head.

"Okay, then. Show me where. We could sneak something in to drink while we're at it. Drink and watch the storm. It'll be a secret, just you and me and—"

"In here." Phillip cut Patrick off and motioned for him to follow. He stepped around a corner and into a room. Blue light flickered from within. "Come on. In here. I'll show you."

Maybe this is a great place to get away from that damn priest and the others. Maybe that's why the village idiot hides down here. Maybe the crazy man will give away the secrets of the Sullivan House, after all. Hopefully, there's something stronger than port in there too.

Patrick grinned, and stepped inside.

TWENTY-SEVEN

SET DIRECTLY IN THE CENTER of the room, a chair with straps and a headboard waited. To one side of the room, long silver trays lined one of the four tiled walls. A case with something that reminded Patrick of cattle prods rested on a separate table. Dials and switches covered the exterior of the paint-chipped box. The interior smelled of burnt wire and rubber. Patrick took a step backward.

"In here. It's fun. Come see." Dragon motioned with his hand for Patrick to join him. "See. Here… here, look at this."

Patrick hesitated. "What is this, Dragon?"

"Don't you trust me? Don't you trust your new friend, Dragon?" Phillip clenched his fists again. One held a cattle prod in it.

"Yes… of course I trust you. I'm just… the air in here smells bad, Dragon."

"You'll forget about it in a minute. Now come in here." Fire flashed behind Phillip's eyes. Patrick moved deeper inside the room, his stare locked on Phillip's. "Now, we're going to play a game. You get to be first. Get on." He nodded to the chair.

"I… I really don't want to be first. You should go."

"I said get on the chair!" Phillips' voice dropped, an entity's voice, compelling Patrick, who jumped onto the odd chair.

"A dentist chair? Why is a dentist's chair in here, Dragon?"

Phillip laughed. "Not a dentist's chair, silly." He secured a leather strap across Patrick's wrist.

"Wait! Stop." Patrick reached over to unleash himself, but the stump only bounced off the leather. "I don't want to do this, Dragon. Let me out of here."

Phillip smiled and secured a strap around an ankle. "Hold still, silly."

"Stop it, Dragon!" Patrick kicked out at Phillip. "Let me go, you freak!"

Suddenly, Phillip stood upright and stared down at Patrick. His expression disappeared and his eyes turned stone cold. "I'm not a freak." With inhuman strength, Phillip grabbed hold of Patrick's other ankle, nearly wrenching his leg out of his hip socket, and secured it with the leather strap. Then, taking hold of Patrick's stump, he held it up and sneered. "This is what happens when you're bad, Patrick. It looks like you haven't paid restitution yet, and now it's my turn!" He slammed Patrick's arm down, securing it just above the stump.

Patrick screamed. "Help! Somebody help me!"

"No one can hear you in here. No one will come for you, anyway—not until you've paid."

His throat began to constrict and Patrick could barely breathe, gasping for air as he panicked. *My arm. If I can wriggle out of this leather, just above the stump...* He twisted against the leather band, but soon discovered that he couldn't break free. His hand had somehow appeared, trapping his arm at the wrist. "What is happening?"

"Oh, good. You're whole again. That's the only way to pay your quittance, anyway."

"Quittance? What the hell does that mean? What are you doing?"

Patrick could hear a low hum coming from the box.

"You know, silly. Your recompense. Can't pay it unless you've got it together, you know. Maybe this time. Fourth time's a charm... or is it third time? I can't remember."

Phillip pulled a strap down tight over Patrick's forehead. His skull slammed against the padded wood block meant to support his head. He couldn't move—except for his eyes, which searched wildly for any way out. He looked above him. Phillip stood at the head of the chair, staring down at him, the psychotic grin spread across his face again. He had donned dark glasses and a rubber apron with matching gloves.

"Okay, we're ready."

"What are you going to do to me?"

Phillip smiled again and touched the pointed needle tips of two cattle prods together. Blue light leapt from their contact point, showering Patrick in sparks. Phillip laughed. "An experiment."

"No! Please!"

"It's my turn." Patrick could see Phillip's lips pouting and his brows knitting together. "I had to wait 'til the others had their turn. But now, it's mine. Maybe it'll work for you this time." He cocked his head, then added, "Does your head still hurt?" Phillip touched the gash on Patrick's scalp.

"No! Stop! Please don't do this!"

Phillip forced a plastic wedge between Patrick's teeth. "You should bite on this. Some people bite off their tongues. It's not on purpose. They can't help it, so it's an accident. But that's usually when they don't use the bite block. See, there's a little hole in it so you can breathe."

Phillip giggled a high, nervous laugh that made Patrick thrash against the straps more vigorously—to no avail. He was restrained and completely vulnerable. He tried to scream, but his voice wouldn't pass the block between his teeth.

"Okey-dokey, arti-chokey. Here we go." Phillip faced Patrick with the cattle prods in hand and placed them on either side of Patrick's head. "Now, watch for the light."

Patrick heard the click of a switch and, instantly, fire pulsed from his brain through every cell in his body. Brilliant blue flashed before his eyes and he could smell hair burning. In that instant, the current passed along his nerve endings, stopping his heart. His chest arched, but the straps held him in place. Patrick could no longer see anything but white—the white-hot of a current that seared his retinas.

In the distance, a shadow appeared. Patrick tried to close his eyes, but they were already shut, spasms clenching his lids together in a steady pulse. He had no control over his own body—except to experience it—the torment that came with an electrical current that continued to burn his insides.

The shadow moved and Patrick watched as it glided to one side. He heard the faint whisper of a voice, Phillip's insanity giggling something, then the shadow moved again. The dark figure shook its head and another whisper followed.

No. His penance is left wanting.

Another jolt from the current sent Patrick's body into spasms. His jaw clenched against the bite block, shattering his teeth with another surge. *Why doesn't this stop?* His heart remained still in his chest. The only pulse in his body came from a box with a switch. *I should be dead. I need to die! Please let me!*

The shadow shook its head. Patrick watched as a smaller shadow took its hand and, together, they disappeared.

"One last try…" The voice was distant, belonging to Phillip.

Another volt shot through Patrick's body, then everything fell to silence.

TWENTY-EIGHT

"IT'S INCOMPREHENSIBLE, REALLY. DID YOU use enough voltage?"

"Yes. I always use enough." Phillip bit off each word as he spoke. "But *she* said he wasn't ready… so I gave him another shock, just in case, and turned off the box."

"Well, it only works on about fifty percent of patients anyway." Father Bielal failed to hide the disappointment in his voice.

"It takes several sessions a week to work. Everyone knows that." Phillip chewed his lower lip and refused to look Father Bielal in the eye.

"You get one chance, Dragon. Only one, just like the rest. Sadly, we're running out of options. Most likely, that's because there were two." The priest shook his head and clasped his hands together inside his tunic sleeves. "Mary will get her turn. I suspect she'll end this."

"That's not fair!" Phillip stomped his foot. "She always wins."

"You had your chance, Dragon. It's time to pass the baton to the next in line." Father Bielal looked down at the charred body on the table. "We'll allow him to awaken properly, then move on. Mary is preparing for him now."

Phillip snorted. "Whatever."

"I'll alert the others and see you in the parlor. We'll need to discuss what happens next. The house won't settle until it's finished."

Phillip glanced overhead, his eyes darting around the room, looking for something unseen. "I understand," he whispered.

Father Bielal nodded, and deep within the walls of the Sullivan House, an entity groaned.

TWENTY-NINE

Patrick slammed his fist against the mirror, shattering the glass into tiny shards. He watched with satisfaction as fragments disappeared into the plush carpeting on the floor. *Someone will step on that… serves them right too!*

"Violence really isn't necessary, Patrick."

"Oh, really? Did you tell *him* that?" Patrick pointed to Phillip, who chewed the inside of his cheek. "Or how about her? She forced acid down my gullet." He pointed to Caroline this time.

"I object! I never forced acid into him." Caroline folded her arms and sneered at Patrick.

"No, it was arsenic," Lizzy snickered.

Patrick shot her a look. "You! This crazy-ass bitch tried to kill me with a hatchet!"

Lizzy began to chuckle.

"Tea?" Mrs. Gillespie stepped into the room, pushing a tea cart filled with porcelain cups, saucers, and a kettle with steam rising from its spout. A tray of tiny sandwiches and dates had been placed next to the setting. "Tempers can best be cooled over a nice cup of tea. Mr. Donovan, do you take sugar?"

Patrick stared incredulously for a moment before storming out of the parlor. His temples still throbbed where the electrodes had been placed, and his finger-tips burned. Without looking, he rubbed his hands together—at least both were still intact. There was no reason to look at the damage Phillip had caused—it would all change, anyway, with time.

"I'm getting out of here. One way or another, I'm getting the hell outta this freaky house!" Patrick whispered, secretly hoping nothing had heard him rant. He glanced along the hallway as if finding evidence of something staring through the wallpaper or from a portrait would confirm he hadn't lost his mind. In truth, he was afraid of what he might find staring back at him from within the walls. Quickly, he shifted his focus ahead.

When he reached the first stairway, he paused. He didn't recognize that staircase, he'd never been in that part of the house before. In fact, Patrick had never seen most of the Sullivan House. *Well, it's time now.*

Given that Patrick knew what lingered behind, anticipating more of the same brought suspicion and, with it, a very bad feeling. Who knew what waited up there—who knew anything about the strange house he found himself in? *Haunted.* Patrick's gut churned. New territory in the Sullivan House felt ominous and full of risks.

There may be a fire escape or a balcony stairwell lead-ing out of the house. It's your only chance, mate. He didn't believe it. The thought unsettled him. He really had no idea what awaited him.

When Patrick reached the landing, the expanse twisted off into several wings. One corridor appeared to be a line of sleeping quarters. Another, service chambers for housing linen and dishware. Obviously, there was another dining area somewhere, but Patrick had had enough of dining rooms and parlors. He could get tea downstairs with the others, if that was what he was after, and it wasn't.

Instead, his gaze followed the farthest corridor. Unable to see more than a few feet beyond the landing, Patrick decided this unused portion of the house had been abandoned long ago. Every inch of this wing looked forgotten. The means for escape would have been forgotten too.

Hope!

He walked into the gloomy annex, glancing to either side of the lengthy corridor for an outlet or portico. With each step, the floor boards groaned, a reminder he was a stranger there. *Perhaps a warning.* Patrick brushed the thought aside and focused on an escape.

Moving deeper into the abandoned wing, he noticed elaborately carved oak doors—some agape on rusted hinges, while others remained closed and shifted in the frames. Nothing looked symmetrical.

"Whoever built this wing needed a level." Patrick was surprised to hear his own voice echoing down the passageway.

He glanced inside one of the open doorways and saw dusty sheers hanging from yellowed windows. The end of a bed peeked from inside the room. An arcane buggy sat at the edge, containing a broken porcelain doll that stared at Patrick with black, hollow eyes.

Not going in there!

Quickly moving past, he made his way farther down the corridor. Ahead, another open door begged he look inside.

Don't do it, Pat!

Unable to contain his curiosity, Patrick glanced in.

Dust motes floated in front of a grimy window that climbed from floor to ceiling. The air smelled stale, acrid. He shrank back, but not before he saw her. Sitting on the edge of the bed, the gaunt, sallow woman he'd seen on the front porch stared back at him. She called out to him.

"Help me."

Patrick froze, staring at her. Death had played an ugly hand with her. He almost felt pity for the woman, until he remembered he'd seen the gravediggers throw her body into a hole.

"You're dead."

She shook her head. *"I just need someone to find where they put it. Help me."*

"In a grave." Patrick cringed. Surely, she didn't want to find her body? "It's… it's probably rotting and…" He swallowed, tasting her decay in his throat. "It's gone."

"It's here. My fix. Somewhere. It's here."

Patrick glanced at the nightstand next to her bed. It was covered with dust—and hypodermic needles. She stood.

"No. I can't help you. No one can." He turned from her and ran. "She's not real, Pat. You saw her body thrown into that grave." He ran into something that shattered with an ear-splitting cacophony. Patrick leapt to one side, away from whatever now threw shards up from the floor. "It's… it's the electricity still playing games with my mind."

When he finally came to the end of the corridor, he froze. Standing above him, nearly fifteen feet high, the framed portrait of a monk stared down at him. Its face was familiar, but the robes and symbols adorning the priest were not.

Patrick tore his gaze from the portrait and rubbed the dust from a nameplate at the base. There he read the inscription in tarnished brass:

Asmodeus Azrael Bielal
Grand Master – Knights of Adrestia
1742 - 1790

Patrick stumbled backward and invisible hands caught him. He spun around but saw only empty darkness. Turning back to face the portrait, he looked up and saw that the monk's eyes were looking down at him.

"Bielal! You bastard!"

He picked up a vase set on a sideboard and readied to throw it at the painting when something caught his eye. To one side, a large leather book lay covered in cobwebs. A familiar symbol engraved on its exterior peeked through the dust covering its surface. Patrick set the vase down and brushed the grime off the front cover.

"*Momento Mori: Et Mortuus Est in Nobis.*" Patrick's breath caught and he glanced up at the portrait of the priest. "You didn't know I could speak Latin, did you?" He looked back at the book and opened the cover. "Well, let's see what the dead have to say, then."

He ran his fingers over the first page. An image of a skull flanked by an hourglass and a goblet on either side took up the entire sheet. It had been drawn with ink and quill.

"Wow!" Patrick leaned in to get a closer look. "This must be worth a fortune!"

He turned the page and studied the fine writing there. Faded colors filled in symbols sketched to resemble life and death. Beneath each image, another phrase in Latin gave the only explanation. Patrick began to read aloud. As he did so, he felt the portrait's stare burning into the back of his head.

"Leave me be, priest. Your secret isn't so cryptic now. No wonder this wing was kept hidden." He glanced up at the portrait momentarily and was met with the dark stare of the monk painted there. "I imagine there are other artifacts hidden within these walls, as well. No wonder Wilkins' store is brimming with so many oddities. He probably steals them from this very wing when you're not looking." Patrick chuckled and the portrait's eyes burned. "You don't scare me, priest." Patrick turned back to the ancient book and began to read again. "*Quaerit poena est peccador*. Retribution seeks the sinner."

Something within the house groaned, but Patrick didn't seem to hear it.

He turned the page and stared at the faces of five men—all dead and positioned as if seated on a church pew. Their eyes were closed and their expressions peaceful as if the hole in each of their foreheads was a blessing. *Perhaps it is… at least to someone.* Patrick snickered and turned the page.

"*Et grata detulerat impius.* The welcomed wicked." He looked at the faded photo. The woman looked no more than sixty, although, with her eyes half-closed, Patrick couldn't be sure. Her mouth was frozen in a sickly grimace that made her look as if she were laughing, even in death's grip. Patrick swallowed back the bile rising to the back of his throat. He knew her face.

"Lizzy."

Below the photograph, the famous rhyme had been scribbled. Patrick didn't need to read the words—he knew it by heart—but couldn't tear his eyes from the page.

Lizzy Borden took an axe, gave her mother forty whacks,

When she'd seen what she had done, gave her father forty-one.

Patrick's mirth disappeared, along with his confidence. He swallowed again and looked closer at the writing next to the dead woman's photo. Scribbled in red along the page borders he read: *Abby 19, Andrew 11. Hatchet.*

"Lizzy?" Patrick turned to look at an empty hallway behind him. "Lizzy? The same Lizzy that's downstairs? The same psycho that whacked me over the head with…"

Patrick froze.

THIRTY

"BUT YOU'RE DEAD." HE LOOKED back at the *memento mori* photograph, noting the date: *June 1927*. Glancing up at the portrait, he continued, "She's freakin' dead! How is she downstairs and dead too…" Just then, Patrick noticed the sinister smile painted on the priest's face. He shook his head, eyes glued to the painting. "No! It can't be."

Turn the page. The thought compelled him, and Patrick quickly turned back to the book, flipping to the next page. More photos of the dead. "'*Momento mori*,'" he whispered.

The next three pages held photos of dead children posed next to very alive siblings or the grieving parents. *Macbre*, was how Patrick could think to describe it. He continued to turn the pages of the book, afraid to see what had been pasted there, but unable to turn away from it at all. In truth, it was an attempt to forget Lizzy's face.

Turning another page, he stared at an entire family lying peacefully on a large bed. Two boys rested next to their father, while the little girl lay between her parents. The only indication of the cause of death was evident on the mother's face—her skull had been crushed just above one eye, which looked bruised and swollen. "Something horrible happened there," Patrick said and flipped to the next page.

"'*Reus est lapis, qui sine dolo causam cognoscere potest.*'" Inked with a guilded pen, the gold letters sparkled in spite of the fading page. Nothing else had been put on the page, except for a few symbols in some lexicon Patrick didn't recognize. "'The guilty atone, the guileless adjudicate.'"

Patrick stared at the page. His spine crawled. "Recompense." His voice nearly failed him as the meaning settled in. Hesitantly, he turned another page.

Photograph after photograph, the vacant eyes of the dead staring up as he turned page after page. He witnessed the familiar faces of those residing in the Sullivan House.

Caroline Shepherd
1897
Murderess – poisoned infant son.

Patrick stared at the noose mark around her neck and remembered the same mark on the woman who called herself by the same name. "She tried to poison me." His skin crawled and he flipped to the next page.

Mary Sanderson
1896
Murderess – cast live infant into fire.

Patrick gasped. "Mary?" The image of her sitting near the fireplace flashed into his mind. "Sick… twisted!" There were no words. He could barely look at her. "You're not so innocent as you appear. You're a monster. I sensed it the minute I met you." He glanced up at the portrait. "You knew all of this and didn't tell anyone! You're as bad as *she* is!"

Turn the page, Patrick.

He turned the page

Donald L. Taylor
aka Hunter
1923
Horse thief, bigamist, murderer – three women,
including wife.

"You dirty, rotten—" Patrick stopped, leaned in to look a little closer at the death image of Hunter. Behind the body in the shadows, two large beasts sat quietly, waiting for their master to awaken.

Patrick rushed to the only window on the landing, praying it looked over the main gates of the estate. Luck was with him, as he could just make out the tall pillars from the front gate in the distance. Atop each one, the same beast sat, staring at anyone who dared to enter. Patrick glanced down at his hand and then to his shin. Both were intact, as was the memory of being eaten.

His dogs! Gargoyles—whatever they were.

Never would Patrick be able to amble out through the front gates. Hunter's creatures would finish their meal. He had to find another way out.

He walked back to the book and flipped another page.

B. M. Gillespie
1820
Yellow Fever – unoffending enlistee.

"What does that mean?" He reread the entry. "She's innocent? Why? Why is she here, then?" Without waiting for an answer, one he really didn't want, he flipped through several more pages to where the paper changed color. It appeared that new pages had been added, creating a new section of the book.

He glanced down at the first page.

Dawn Alba
2017
Murderess – neglect.

"The addict." Patrick's voice had dropped to a whisper. He looked behind him at the empty hallway where he had seen her sitting on the bed. "She's in there… here… she's dead. I saw them throw her body in the hole." He glanced at the window, his thoughts on the cemetery just outside and the freshly dug grave there. "How…?"

With shaky fingers, he turned the page again. Looking down at the crisp, white paper, Patrick felt his knees grow weak and he stumbled backward. His vision narrowed to just the name written there in fresh ink:

Patrick Donovan
2017
Murderer – wife and daughter shot with handgun.

THIRTY-ONE

"THE FIRST TIME IS ALWAYS very unsettling… to see your name on the ledger."

Patrick spun around and faced the monk. "Bielal! You mother f—"

Father Bielal held his hand up. Patrick couldn't breathe—he couldn't speak. "We advise you to avoid such language in a sacred place such as this." The priest began to pace, walking first to the window to glance out before sauntering back to Patrick. "Consider yourself, Mr. Donovan." He dropped his hand and Patrick gasped. The monk kept his back to Patrick as he stared out the window. "Still, I understand your dismay."

"My dismay? Is that what you call it?" Patrick choked out each word. "What the hell is this? And why the hell is my name on here?" He slapped the open book with the back of one hand.

"That is a ledger." Father Bielal's brows knitted together as he stepped up protectively to the book. The smell of mothballs and frankincense assaulted Patrick's senses. He took a step backward.

"Why is my name in there? A ledger of what?"

"The dead, Mr. Donovan."

Patrick began to pace. "I'm not dead, you fool!"

The priest grew quiet and his voice dropped. "We all die eventually, Mr. Donovan. This book contains the names of those who have met the requirements for forgiveness—their retribution."

Patrick stopped in his tracks. "For what?"

"Sin." Father Bielal paused and Patrick felt his face blanch. He recalled the words written below his name. "Yes, Mr. Donovan. You have sins you need to make restitution for. That can only come through retribution."

"From whom?"

Father Bielal smiled. "From the victims."

"Victims? I'm the victim here! You and your little band of special effects techies have messed with my head long enough. I don't know how you do it, but it's clever enough to make a person believe this is all real."

Father Bielal turned to look at Patrick. "This isn't real?"

"No! And you can stop acting like I'm going to buy into whatever you're selling. You're not scaring me away from buying this place. I'm not dead, I have no retribution to pay, and there's nothing in my past that's any of your business! My attorney is going to have a heyday with this place… with you, when I get out of here. Speaking of *you*…" Marching back to the book, Patrick flipped through the pages. "I don't see your name in there."

"Alas, my retribution is visible for all to see." He reached up to the brass nameplate on the frame and rubbed the remaining dust away. "You read Latin, I understand?"

"Yeah, but I must have missed that."

"Come, see here. You'll understand my destiny better." The priest motioned for Patrick to join him, but Patrick refused. Bielal motioned again. "Please, look at this. I've nothing to hide and you've nothing to fear."

Patrick paused to allow Bielal to move away before stepping up to the portrait. He leaned in to stare at the inscription again.

Asmodeus Azrael Bielal
Grand Master – Knights of Adrestia
1742 - 1790
nefas animo iniquo iudicio

"'Unholy judgement, unrighteous intent?'" Patrick looked up at the portrait and then to Father Beilal. "What are you?"

"I am like you—forever destined to remain in this house until my retribution is paid in full."

Patrick backed away. "What happened? I mean, what did you do?"

"I killed the innocent."

"You did what?" Patrick shook his head and took another step away from the painting. "Why me? My intent was only to buy this nasty place. I think I've changed my mind, though. I need to find Wilkins… let him know the sale is off."

The priest chuckled. "Ah, Wilkins. Now there's an interesting fellow."

"Yeah, what's his deal, anyway? Why isn't he in here?" Patrick motioned to the book. "He's obviously a con artist… a crook."

"Like the rest of us, Wilkins' retribution is sealed upon his head."

"Sealed upon his head? Wha… what do you mean?"

Bielal moved to a chair next to the window and took a seat. Crossing his hands on his lap, he looked like he had just settled in for a long, drawn-out convocation. He sighed. "You see, Patrick, when someone commits an act—any act—that causes harm to another soul, absolution is required. It doesn't matter who or what is offended—the victim can be people, animals, nature—a requirement for retribution is always attached. It's been the discussion of holy men for centuries."

"In other words, the sinner must pay a price for his sins. Yeah, I remember hearing something about that in Sunday school as a little kid. Didn't believe it, then… don't believe it now."

Beilal chuckled. "Which is why you are here. You have much to absolve from your past."

"*That* is none of your business! Who or what I injure in life is *my* problem."

"There have been many in your past—and not all human."

Patrick began to pace, his gaze bouncing from the monk to the open book. "You mean to tell me I have to pay a price for carving my initials in a tree?"

Beilal nodded. "I'm afraid so, my son."

"I'm not 'your son,' and you don't know scripture very well. The Bible says I'm saved from all of that."

"Indeed, you are." Father Beilal tucked both hands inside his robe and shifted in his seat. The chair looked like it might collapse under his weight but held. "Scripture is truth. But you still have to pay your part—make up for your contribution to the injury, as it were. And yes, you must pay retribution for carving your initials into a tree, if that causes pain and injury to the tree. Only the tree knows how much it suffers from your actions—hence, it becomes your judge. It's a living entity, just like you… like us all have been at one time."

"Doesn't fit me." Patrick gestured theatrically. "I'm not dead."

"Not yet, Mr. Donovan. But your retribution has not yet been fully paid."

Patrick stopped pacing and stared down the priest. "You keep saying that! Retribution for sin. I heard you the first time. But for what? What did I ever do to you… or this stupid, old house?"

Bielal shot him a dark look. "Caution, Patrick. I've warned you before about thinking carefully before speaking."

"What? The dead will turn in their graves?" Patrick laughed hysterically, but there was no mirth in his tone. "I've done nothing!"

"You saw the writing beneath your name, Mr. Donovan. It said '*Murder*,' if my recollection serves me." Patrick stopped laughing and the priest nodded. "I see you recall the sin. It's always much more difficult to resolve the issue when the sinner cannot remember what he… or she… has done."

Opening his mouth, Patrick tried to speak, but his voice failed him. He remained where he stood, unable to move, searching for an escape. "I'm not ready for any retribution. You have no proof. I was aquitted."

Father Beilal smiled. "Man's courts are not spiritual houses of justice. It's very obvious that you are not complete yet. Your retribution may be very lengthy and distressing at the rate you're going, Mr. Donovan. I would suggest a change of attitude to begin with."

"I'm not falling for this, Beilal. You and your ridiculous Knights of Algae, or whatever they are, can go to hell."

In that instant, the priest threw back his head and laughed. It sounded deep and otherworldy, echoing through the arterial hallways of the Sullivan House. When he had stopped, his eyes blazed as they stared at Patrick. "This is my hell. I am the son of purgatory, whose recompense it is to mete out justice on those who've wronged mankind, as I did."

Patrick began to tremble. "You're not my judge," he whispered.

"No…" Bielal's eyes softened. "Thankfully, that duty falls to the victims."

Just then, as if confirming the truth, the walls vomited its shadows and Patrick found himself surrounded by spirits. Their blank eyes stared, unfocussed, as they inched forward.

"Stop! Stop this, Beilal!"

"These are your judges here." The priest beckoned, and Patrick watched as Sarah and Heather materialized. "They determine when your retribution has been met. Until then, you continue."

"How? How do…?"

Bielal stood. "Each of six chosen souls, waiting for their own release, mete out punishment in hopes your retribution is met. Once that miraculous event takes place, their souls are free to move on. Retribution and restitution has been meted out, and they are no longer bound to this world."

"But how…?"

"Only the victims decide when you have achieved that."

"Punishment? From those freaks back there… in the dining room?"

Beilal nodded.

"No!"

"It's the destiny you chose by your actions, Mr. Donovan."

"Then, I… I chose Mrs. Gillespie. She can mete out justice, or whatever it is, to me. After that, I'm getting the hell outta here!" Patrick glanced at the ghosts and Sarah's expression shifted. He reached out to the little girl. "Oh, Sarah, sweetie. Don't cry, baby."

Bielal walked slowly toward the open book. "Mrs. Gillespie is an unusual resident. She joined us voluntarily, consumed by guilt when she could not stop the spread of the Yellow Fever that took the lives of six hundred and sixty-six souls. She remains here to serve only and ease the burden of others so that she may rid herself of guilt."

"Six-six-six? That's the number of people that died of Yellow Fever? Here?"

Father Beilal stared off into the distance, lost in another time. "Yes. So tragic. Mrs. Gillespie was one of those numbers, poor soul. Hopefully, one day, she can be released from guilt's grip to go be with her loved ones in peace."

Patrick swallowed. "You… you said Mary was next. She burned her baby alive. What… what is she going to do to me?"

Snapping to, Bielal shrugged. "That is of Mary's chosing. She's become so obsessed with fire since she's arrived… I hope it's not too much for you to bear."

Patrick looked past Bielal to the ghosts. Behind the priest, the spirit shook her head. "Heather, please.

Stop this!" Patrick choked on the words and felt tears dampen his cheeks.

The spirit shook her head again.

"Heather…"

Again, the spirit said, *No*.

He shifted his attention back to the monk. "I'm not doing this!" Patrick pointed to Beilal. "Not doing this!"

He turned away, headed toward the darkened hallway, and a tiny voice whispered, "*Oh, daddy!*"

THIRTY-TWO

A STENCH—MOLDY, ROTTED, A SCENT that only belongs to ancient decay—hit Patrick's nostrils as he ran. The hallway remained dark, an almost impenetrable blackness that light barely pricked its way through. He blinked a few times, hoping that would clear his vision. Behind him, plodding footsteps echoed, and he wondered if he was alone. This wing remained abandoned for a reason, apparently. Wispy brume blew past him, and with it, the sound of a voice warning him to turn back.

"No!"

Someone weeping, a hollow, mournful cry, howled distantly. Patrick stumbled at the sound of it but caught his balance in time. Falling would surely be his end—he could not let that happen. With a new resolve, he lengthened his strides.

"She's waiting for you…"

"No! Dammit!"

"Waiting… go back… face them."

"I said, before, I'm not doing this!"

Patrick rounded a corner and the walls shifted. Overhead, an enormous chandelier swung—a crystal pendulum waiting to rain glass over anything below. The wind howled, and Patrick stopped, looking through the shadows to get his bearings. To one side, floor-to-ceiling windows glowed with the steely indigo of a cloud-covered moonlight. With each gust of wind, sheers billowed outward, grasping at him. He moved aside and looked for a way out.

Just ahead of him, marble statues bled black from their eyes and mouths. To one side, tombstones toppled to their sides, waiting to mark the dead. Riddling the walls, open vaults yawned, anticipating corpses yet to be placed ther. Death permeated the house throughout.

"A columbarium," Patrick whispered. Retracing his steps, he backed away, then turned to leave the macbre refectory, but there was no hallway—no entrance and no exit. The walls had closed behind him. He was trapped inside the great hall used to contain the dead and hold their recepticles in repose. "No… no! There has to be a way out!"

Patrick ran. His shoulder smacked into the marble plaque covering the crypt not more than fifty feet from where he had started. The sheers billowed and moonlight danced across weatherworn writing.

> *Robert Woolston*
> *died age 63 in 1887*
> *Butchered by son*

A skull and crossbones had been etched into the stone. Patrick stumbled back and looked for another way out. He rushed toward a shadowed area of the chamber. There, he met another wall.

"No!"

Patrick smacked the marble with his open palms. Suddenly, the plaque crumbled and Patrick fell forward, landing on rubble and wood. Dust rose, nearly suffocating him while the dank stench of rotted tissue made him gag. He scrambled to his knees and found himself staring, not at rubble, but at a broken coffin and bones. A skull lolled to one side, staring at Patrick with hollow black holes for eyes. Its hair, matted to the top, splayed outward at the first breath of air making its way into the crypt.

Patrick cried out and fell from the opening, landing on the stone floor of the columbarium. He gasped and crawled away from the tomb, while the skeleton's eyes followed him. Desperate to get out of there, he searched the chamber again, scanning for any break in the darkness—a sign of escape.

On the opposite side, he spotted a sliver of light.

"There! Wait!" he shouted as if someone would hear him from within the light.

Without waiting for a response, Patrick ran to it and found the source—an open door, cracked just enough to send a becon to summon him. He pulled the oak door open and leapt into the light.

A sudden blast from an incinerator made him recoil, turning his face away from the heat. Almost immediately, his lungs burned, as well. The retort's door was open, and a slate table was extended, waiting for its next body.

"How did I get…?" He shied away, turning to face the door closing behind him. An instant later, he heard the click of the lock. Again, Patrick found no escape and began pounding on the heavy oak door.

"No one can hear you."

Patrick jumped and turned to see Mary walking softly toward the oven's waiting table. She smiled and shook her head.

"You leave me alone!" Patrick's voice failed him.

"It will all be over soon. I promise." Mary's voice sounded gentle, almost as if she were singing a lullabye. She looked at the fire, then back to Patrick. "Have you never seen a funeral pyre before?"

"Stay away!"

"It's my turn now. You need to be fair." She patted the slate tenderly, apparently oblivious to its temperature. "Come, lie back and relax."

"No!"

Something groaned within the walls. Patrick looked around for the source but saw nothing except ash-covered tile. Eyes wild, he looked back at Mary.

"The house wants you to get in."

THIRTY-THREE

"YOU LEAVE ME ALONE!"

The house groaned again. Mary glanced at the same tiled walls and smiled. "You haven't recompensed your victims yet. You still can, though… the house wants you to. Me too." She sounded almost innocent, but Patrick knew otherwise. Of all the souls within the Sullivan House, Mary was its worst monster.

"Just… just shoot me or something like that. That'll work. I'm already sorry for… for what I did." Even Patrick didn't believe the words spewing from his mouth.

Mary glanced behind him at the slit used for an observation window. He followed her gaze and saw Heather's face, wispy, pale, on the other side of the glass. She shook her head.

"Apparently, you're not. She says so."

Patrick rushed up to the window, pounding with his fists against the heavy pane. There was no sound as he beat the glass. "Heather. Please, honey. Tell them how sorry I am."

The ghost shook its head.

"See? I think someone suggested an 'eye for an eye' approach for you, but the counsel said shooting you, the way you shot her and the little one, would be too easy. No suffering for your sins."

"Heather, please, baby. Please! Give me another chance. Let me make up for it, but not this way."

The ghost shook its head, and the walls groaned.

"You're making the house angry. You need to get in." Mary began tapping her foot.

Patrick turned to face her. If he couldn't force his way out, he might be able to talk Mary out of it, somehow. He was always good at conning his way around a problem. He glanced back at Heather, but she was gone.

"She left. She doesn't want the little one to watch."

"Look. I need some answers." Patrick stepped forward and the house groaned again.

Mary shook her head. "I can't. Sorry. You didn't give them a chance, and you didn't let them ask any questions before you murdered them. Fair is fair."

"Answer just one question for me, just one…" He looked at the fire. "…first." Another groan. Patrick looked up at the ceiling and then the walls. "It's the least you can give me!" Patrick shouted at the house.

Mary stared at the walls for a long moment, then nodded. "Okay. One question."

"Why? Why this?" He gestured to the incinerator.

"I told you, recompense to your victims for what you did. You just wasted your question." Mary snorted and rolled her eyes. "You're not very smart, are you?"

"You didn't let me finish, Mary."

She looked at him with wide eyes. "Oh?"

"Why didn't the other times work? I mean, like when Lizzy bludgeoned me with the hatchet or when Caroline poisoned me? And those dogs…"

"Grotesques. They're not dogs. Hunter gets very angry when you call them dogs."

Patrick forced back the sneer that threatened his lips. He had distracted her. Perhaps the Sullivan House too. Refusing to acknowledge the house's presence, he kept Mary in his focus. "I don't even know what a grotesque is. Whatever they were, they tried to eat me."

Mary grinned. "They do that because they're grotesques. Gargoyles spit water. Grotesques guard and attack when they feel threatened."

"How did I threaten…?"

"You were on the property and trying to escape. Everyone knew it. Donald Taylor hunts. That's why we call him Hunter, you know."

Patrick nodded. "Yes, I know Hunter's nickname."

"Well, he sent the grotesques to hunt you down, bring you back. Then the house decided to keep you alive so you could pay your recompense." She glanced at the flames. "You better get in now."

Patrick remembered how the beasts had stopped when he had crawled up the staircase to the front door. "So that's why…?"

"Yes, now get on the table. It's time."

"No, wait—you didn't answer my question. Why did I survive the others?"

Mary's face lit up. "Oh! That's easy. Because you weren't absolved yet. She hadn't decided you were finished, and the counsel listens to her when it comes to *your* recompense."

"Who?"

Mary pointed to someone behind him. He turned to look and saw, standing inside the door, the ghosts of his wife and daughter. Heather shook her head again and the walls groaned.

"It's time, now."

Invisible hands grasped hold of Patrick. Terror swept through him as he watched Heather's ghost and Mary close in. Whispering voices drowned out his thoughts—and Patrick knew he needed to think fast.

"Wait! You can't burn me alive. Not while I'm alive!"

"Well, yes, I can."

"Wait! Stop, please! You still didn't answer my question, Mary." He looked at the ghosts and then to the walls. "I just need answers, then I'll go."

Mary sighed. "It's too late."

Patrick felt the unseen hands digging into his flesh. "But who is this counsel and why only me? Why aren't you in there?" The flames lapped at the opening as if licking its lips, waiting to consume him.

Mary stiffened. "The counsel says I'm not finished yet. I did something terrible, they said. They called me a monster because I… I… burned my baby in the fire."

Though the words were remorseful, Patrick saw no emotion as Mary spoke. "You are a monster," he whispered.

"Just like you. You murdered your baby too."

Patrick could not move. The hands held him fast and his voice had failed him. No argument—he *had* murdered Heather and Sarah in a desperate moment. It was true. But the courts had pardoned him on a technicality. "What about the counsel?"

"That's a new question."

Suddenly, Patrick was flat on his back, his body strapped to the slate. Flames lapped at his head, and he felt the heat beginning to scorch the top of his head. Blisters rose instantly and he cried out.

With a quick shove, Mary slid him into the furnace. He was aware of it all and opened his mouth to scream, but the fire took hold of him first. For just a moment, the flames stroked his skin, coaxing plasma to boil while the fleshy parts dried to leather, and each muscle contracted—then charred. All of his tissue vaporized and the smell of burnt hair lingered just before Patrick's bones crumbled.

THIRTY-FOUR

"THIS COUNCIL IS NOW IN session."

Three raps of a gavel sounded, and the congregation sat down. Heather took her seat, along with Sarah, at the side of the Grand Master's cathedra. Everyone seated at the dais stared down at the gathering below. In front of the podium, a glass case exposing bones and ash rested on a black silk serviette.

"Heather Donovan presents her case to the counsel on behalf of herself and her daughter, Sarah. They have observed the recompense of the sinner and have made a decision."

The grand master nodded to Heather, and she stood, clutching little Sarah's hand. She cleared her throat. "I saw no remorse, only anger, and desire to escape restitution." She lifted her chin slightly. "He is not absolved."

"This is the weapon?" The Grand Master motioned and a robed man stood, holding a revolver by the butt, the barrel pointed downward.

A low rumble echoed from the cathedral domed ceiling as the audience murmured amongst themselves. Heather nodded and sat back down, then glanced at the Grand Master, who rapped his gavel again.

"It seems Mr. Patrick Donovan remains *labile immotus*, despite the many attempts at reclamation for his soul. He remains unrepentant at heart. Is there anyone present who can attest otherwise?" The Grand Master scanned the crowd.

Heads were bowed as the members murmured amongst themselves again. Slowly, one by one, each member looked up at the Grand Master, shaking their heads *no*.

"Deposit the weapon with Mr. Wilkins. He'll depose of it per policy."

Heather's expression remained sullen, though a flicker of approval flashed behind her eyes as she watched them.

"She whom none can escape, the Mother who punishes human injustice, which is a transgression of the natural right of order, declares it. And, as witness to all that has transpired, and by the vote of this counsel, it is the unanimous decision of the Knights of Adrestia that Patrick Donovan resume payment in retribution for his soul. He shall be turned over to the Sullivan House for rebirth."

A smack of the gavel signaled the end of the conference. Each of the members stood and waited as the Grand Master descended the rostrum and made his way to the glass case containing Patrick's remains. He was joined by two other men. Draped around each of their necks was silk embroidered with symbols that matched the caps and sashes worn by the others there. The Knights of Adrestia were indeed impressive to behold, an army for justice—even within the walls of the Sullivan House.

Carefully slipping a set of poles into openings on both sides, the men shouldered the glass case containing Patrick's remains and carried it out. The Grand Master led the way, trailed by Heather and Sarah. Each row of knights took its place in the procession, walking out of the massive gathering hall and into the cemetery. Waiting next to an open grave, Caroline, Phillip, Mary, Hunter, and Lizzy watched their arrival, with Jeb and Ben standing with shovels in hand. Only Father Bielal and Mrs. Gillespie remained on the porch, watching from a distance.

When they had gathered at the grave, the Grand Master glanced at Father Bielal, who nodded. "Let's begin, then." He took up a handful of dirt and placed it into Heather's open palm. "You are the one who decides, my dear. You are the one who must begin this."

He patted her fist, smiled, and stepped away. Heather stared at the glass case that had been set to one side. Glancing at her daughter, she placed a portion of the dirt into Sarah's little hand before looking back at the bones encased in glass. Her focus moved to the grave. Lying in wait, a wooden coffin had been set in the bottom, its lid resting to one side. Her face soured and she looked up at the knights in red silk, then nodded.

Each took a side and rolled the case upside down, spilling the contents into the open casket. There would be no ceremony, no respectful laying of the dead to rest. Not this time. Patrick would not rest. The Sullivan House would see to that. He would be reborn from ash to rise again and meet his restitution all over again.

And Heather would watch.

She waited until Jeb and Ben had set the lid on the coffin. Once in place, the men hopped out of the grave and resumed their position away from the rest, shovels in hand.

Holding her clenched fist over the grave, she dropped the dirt onto the coffin, then nodded for Sarah to do the same. One by one, each of the Knights of Adrestia tossed a handful of dirt onto Patrick's coffin, whispered something in Latin, then turned and walked out of the cemetery. The last to throw was Mary, who smiled and whispered her own thoughts.

"I'll be waiting for you."

As they walked through the cemetery, Sarah looked back at the grave and tugged her mother's hand. "Why does Daddy stay there?"

There was only a small pause before she gave her answer.

"Because his chest doesn't rise anymore."

THIRTY-FIVE

The sun had set early and the skies grown dark the night Patrick was put into the ground. No one remained behind—none except for the gravediggers. Not even a marker had been prepared. They wouldn't need one. Not for this grave.

Benjamin tossed another shovel full of dirt in and stomped it down firmly. "Almost done."

"Pack it tight, Benj. We don't want it too easy for 'im!" Jeb threw back his head and laughed.

Benjamin nodded and repeated the process, tromping down the dirt a little more this time. Then, catching his breath, he leaned against his shovel, crossed his heels, and stared at Jeb. "Why do you think it's so hard for this one?"

Jeb shrugged. "Dunno. Maybe he's just stubborn.

"Maybe." Benjamin looked at the freshly filled grave. "Do you think it'll be soon?"

"Naw." Jeb shook his head and stuck the tip of his shovel into the dirt, then spat tobacco juice from the side of his mouth. The soft earth instantly turned dark where it landed. "I heard when they get burned up and there's nothin' left but bones, it takes a while." He glanced down at the dirt and spat again. "I heard they feel every cell in their body come back, like being burned again, only backwards."

Benjamin nodded. "I heard that too."

Both men stared at the grave for a moment, contemplating just what that meant. After a while, Jeb took a swig from a flask and handed it to Benjamin.

"It'll likely take 'im a while to figure out what's going on."

"Yeah… buried alive!" Benjamin tipped back the flask again, laughing.

Jeb nodded. "Yup. Buried alive. When he figures it out, he'll start scratchin'. That's why we don't nail the lid on the coffin, you know. So they can dig their way out."

"If they can dig their way out. How many coffin lids have you seen with marks on the inside, Jeb? Bloodied marks from fingernails, I heard."

"Lots!" Jeb puffed out his chest. "I've seen lots like that. Bloody scratches on the inside of the coffins from them diggin' their way out. Once, I found a whole fingernail stuck in the wood."

"No!"

"Yup!"

"And this one didn't get a bell."

The gravediggers picked up their shovels and walked toward the iron gate. Neither looked back at the graveyard. Each man shared a drink, clapping one another on the back for another job well done. Stories exchanged, both men walked the long path to the road leading from the house. Neither noticed the crack of lightning overheard or heard the deep groan of an entity as it watched them leave.

A single light flickered in the window of the great mansion, bidding welcome to lost souls. Behind it, a monk in ancient robes smiled. Within, the Sullivan House turned dark eyes to the graveyard, content to wait.

POST MORTEM

WILKINS HEARD THE BELLS FROM the upstairs storage room announcing a new customer. He turned his head and sighed. It would be a long day with so many interruptions. Gently, he placed the revolver on a table and stood for a moment to inspect it.

"Hello? Wilkins?"

Her voice was familiar. After nodding his approval, he turned and whispered, "*Memento mori—novi ut hos pitis nostri.*"

Not many years ago, the stairs down to the main floor were easy to navigate. These days, Wilkins felt his age with the descent. Rubbing his back, he entered the enormous room filled with antiquities, feeling very much like he belonged there. He forced a smile.

"Good evening, Melissa. What brings you here?"

"Hello, Mr. Wilkins. Research, of course."

"Ah, I've just tagged a new entry. Cleaning it for display now."

"From the Sullivan House?"

"Yes. Would you like to see it?"

Melissa glanced up to where Wilkins had been. She shook her head. "No, thank you. Maybe another time."

"Very well then. It's a lovely piece—a murder weapon, I've been told."

They exchanged looks and Melissa shifted her gaze to the vast collection of weaponry decorating the wall behind him. A blank spot had been prepped with hooks—the new procurement, she assumed. She pointed to a curved sword hanging to one side.

"That's lovely. It's also new, is it not?"

Wilkins glanced over his shoulder at the cutlass and smiled. "Yes. It came in just last week. 18th century, Scottish, recovered from Newfoundland and brought in by a young man claiming it had been in his family." Wilkins shook his head slowly. "The treasures this generation choose to part with."

"I agree. Such a loss… for them, anyway."

Wilkins cocked his head and smiled at her. "I suspect, you are not here to discuss ancient weapons, however. What can I help you find, Melissa?"

Melissa returned his smile and pushed an ancient book across the counter to within Wilkins' reach. "The volume should be updated."

"I see." Wilkins nodded.

"And this needs to be included in your private collection." Melissa set a bundle wrapped in velvet next to the book. "Not for sale, as you know."

Wilkins carfully removed the velvet wrap and stared down at a dagger. "19th century?"

"Most likely."

"It's been well cared for." Wilkins ran his finger over the blade that had been coated with a waxy substance. "Someone took great care to make certain this knife was preserved."

Melissa stared at it, nodding. "Yes. There is a great deal of history behind that blade."

Wilkins took out a loupe from a drawer and held it to an eye. Leaning in, he stared at the weapon through the lens. Melissa waited, hoping she'd get a turn with it. "There's damage to the blade. It looks like its been well used."

"Yes."

"The guard has traces of… stain, it looks like. I don't think it's rust. But then, I'm not an expert."

After a moment, he stood upright and handed her the magnifying glass. "See for yourself."

Melissa took the loupe and following Wilkins' example, staring closely at the knife. "There, I see it too. I wonder how this could have been missed."

"Maybe fate played a hand. Maybe the 'experts' thought they were looking at rust." He snickered and shook his head. "People see what they want to see, don't they?"

"Well, these nicks along the edges are noticeable, even to the untrained eye." She handed the loupe back to him. "Thank you."

"What does your untrained eye think caused that damage to such a sharp blade?"

She glanced from the dagger to Wilkins and back down to the blade again. "Bone."

Wilkins nodded. "This will be kept safely away, along with the rest. I'll make my notes in the book and have it back to the library before the end of the day." He patted the leather-bound book.

"Thank you. It cannot survive outside of the vault for long, as you know."

"Of course, Melissa."

She nodded and turned to walk out of the shop. As she reached the door, Wilkins stopped her.

"May I ask one question of you?" Without waiting for permission, Wilkins continued. "Can you tell me just who this knife belonged to?"

Melissa paused. Without turning to face him, she said, "The next resident of Sullivan House. You'll see his name in the book. I believe his nickname was, 'Ripper.'"

Wilkins watched as she walked out. Then, staring at the knife again, he smiled and said, "There is much you will have to tell us. Your story will be one of interest to many. I will be listening, my friend." He wrapped the blade, tucked it under his arm, and walked back into the darkness.

*****

That evening, lightning illuminated the cemetery at Sullivan House. Dark eyes stared out from its gable windows, waiting, watching.

No one heard the scratching noise coming from beneath Patrick's grave.

Enjoy Other Books By

Doce Blant Publishing
www.DoceBlant.com

Alys
by Kiri Callaghan

Hardbound ISBN: 978-0-9978913-8-6
Paperback ISBN: 978-0-9978913-9-3
ePub ISBN: 978-0-9984294-0-3

The Déjà vu Chronicles
by Marti Melville
Midnight Omen (book 1)
Hardbound ISBN: 978-0-9971023-3-8
Paperback ISBN: 978-0-9971023-4-5
ePub ISBN: 978-0-9971023-5-2
Library of Congress Control Number:
2016906558

The Tales of Barnacle Bill: Skeleton Krewe
by Barnacle Bill Bedlam

Hardbound ISBN: 978-0-9967622-3-6
Paperback ISBN: 978-0-9967622-2-9
ePub ISBN: 978-0-9967622-4-3

The Next Victim
by Cutter Slagle

Hardbound ISBN: 978-0-9967622-6-7
Paperback ISBN: 978-0-9967622-5-0
ePub ISBN: 978-0-9967622-7-4

'Til Death
by Cutter Slagle

Hardbound ISBN: 978-0-9978913-0-0
Paperback ISBN: 978-0-9978913-1-7
ePub ISBN: 978-0-9978913-2-4
Library of Congress Control Number:
2016949335

Never Surrender
by Deanna Jewel

Hardbound ISBN: 978-0-9971023-0-7
Paperback ISBN: 978-0-9971023-1-4
ePub ISBN: 978-0-9971023-2-1